IF YOU COULD READ MY MIND
A NICHOLAS TURNER NOVEL
BY
T. M. BILDERBACK

I0549772

Copyright © 2009 by T. M. Bilderback

To Stephanie, my own little angel.

Chapter 1

WHAFUCK? thought Nicholas Turner.

Something woke him up, because he was looking at the ceiling. It needed painting. It had needed painting for some time, but if it was waiting for him to do it, it would have a long wait. His life sucked enough without having paint added to it, and bright colors did not match any mood he'd had lately. The dust, spider webs, and water stains did match his moods, however, so that was the end of that.

He was lying on his back, in the same position that he had passed out. At least he hadn't spilled bourbon all over himself - there hadn't been any left in the bottle when he toppled over.

His head felt as if the 3rd Infantry was marching through it.

Why do I do it? he thought to himself. *I know how I'm going to feel afterwards, so why do I do it?*

Of course, he knew the answer. And the binges had been few and far between lately, so it must be getting less painful.

Riiiight...

Twelve years ago, Nicholas Turner had been a cop, and a good one. He had just been promoted to Detective - the youngest on the force ever to be promoted that quickly, and he had a promising career ahead of him. He had been married to the love of his life, Jane, for a year and a half, and he was on top of the world.

Two months after his promotion, he came home from work to candles on the dining room table, and Janey in the kitchen cooking his favorite meal, with a smile on her face.

"What's up, sugarpie?" he said, coming up behind her and nuzzling the back of her neck. "Did you overdraw the checking account again?"

She turned to him and pushed him away. "You'll find out, Mr. Detective. Now, go change clothes and wash up for dinner."

After dinner, Nicholas put down his napkin. "All right, what's going on?"

Jane smiled at him. "How do you feel about being a father?"

"Well, I know that we've talked about it, and..." Realization dawned on him. "You're pregnant?"

She nodded, smiling.

He couldn't wipe the grin off of his face. He went to her, took her in his arms, and kissed her. Then, he held her close for a minute, and kissed her again. He got a mischievous idea.

With mock seriousness, he looked into her eyes and said, "Are you sure it's mine?"

She threw her napkin at him.

Later, in bed, he asked her how far along she was.

"The doctor said I was about two months. That only gives us about seven months to get the guest room changed into a nursery."

The next four months were the happiest in both their lives. They fixed the nursery as best as they could without knowing the sex of the baby. They child-proofed most of the house. They told both sets of parents, and told Nicholas's sister, Melissa. They asked Nicholas's best friend, Marcus Moore, who went into the FBI after he and Nicholas graduated college, to be the baby's godfather. They chose the final baby names - Stephen Nicholas if it was a boy, and Madeline Louise if it was a girl.

In the second week of her sixth month of pregnancy, Jane miscarried. Nicholas was on duty, and got the message while at work. When he arrived at the hospital, the miscarriage was already over. The doctor met him in the waiting room with even more bad news.

The baby would not have survived even if it had made it to a full term. Jane had ovarian cancer, and it was a rapid-growing, virulent strain. She would not be leaving the hospital. She died three weeks later.

Nicholas was devastated. After the funeral, Melissa wanted him to come spend a few days at her house, but he refused. Marcus offered to stay with Nicholas for a while, but he turned him down, too. He drove home alone.

Inside, he went to the liquor cabinet, took out the bottle of Jack Daniels, and went into the nursery. He sat beside the never-to-be-used crib in the rocking chair that would never rock his child to sleep, and drank himself unconscious, tears drying on his cheeks. He stayed that way, drunk and crying, alternating between the nursery and what used to be his and Jane's bedroom, for three days.

On the fourth day, still feeling the effects of his binge, he returned to work. Every cop on the force offered condolences. He thanked them all, and sat at his desk. As he began reviewing his cases, he occasionally snuck a quick nip from the flask he brought from home. Occasionally, he would write something in one of the case files, or make a follow-up phone call.

Many of the cops he worked with noticed what he was doing...but the general feeling was that Nicholas would snap out of it soon.

After a week of desk duty, he was called out on a case. Two patrolmen had answered a domestic abuse call, and he was assigned to lead the case. When he arrived at the scene, a young woman had been beaten severely by her live-in boyfriend. Her six-month-old son also had two large bruises on his face.

The woman told Nicholas that her boyfriend was the child's father. He had been drinking, and growing more belligerent as he drank. When their son awoke from his nap and began crying, the boyfriend had punched the boy twice before she could intervene. When she got between them, he began punching her. Then he left.

Nicholas asked where he might find the man. The woman named a local bar and gave him a description.

Telling one of the two patrolmen to stay with her and to take her wherever she wanted to go, he took the other patrolman with him to the bar.

The boyfriend was sitting at the bar drinking. Nicholas walked up to him, showed the man his badge, and told him that he was under arrest. As he handcuffed the man, he told him his rights. The man was smirking.

"Bitch got what she had coming," the man said.

Nicholas and the patrolman escorted the man from the bar.

"Shoulda given her more," the man said, as he was being escorted. "Fuckin' brat's gotta learn who wears the pants in the house. Shoulda drowned the little fucker when he was born. Him and his fuckin' whore bitch mama!"

During this tirade, Nicholas made no comment. But, instead of leading the man to the patrol car, he continued on to the alley beside the bar.

"Where the fuck you takin' me, pig?" the man asked.

Nicholas slammed the man against the brick wall of the bar with all his strength, cutting off his comments in mid-sentence. Then, he began systematically punching the man, alternating between face, stomach, and kidneys. He only stopped when the patrolman pulled him away. The man collapsed onto the ground, bleeding and unconscious.

The meeting with the chief of detectives was short.

"Turner, you got lucky. The patrolman backed up your story that the man was violently resisting arrest, so the story is two against one. But, I cannot have this type of behavior in my detectives." The chief took off his glasses and looked at Nicholas. "But you and I both know that the case's circumstances made you angry because of your personal tragedy. Christ, Turner, you nearly beat that man to death!"

He paused. "The next few comments are me to you, off the record. I don't blame you for what you did. The man was trash, and had it coming. And what I've got to do to you as punishment goes against everything I believe in, but, understand that I've got no choice - this came from higher up than me." He put his glasses back on and looked at Nicholas. "Detective Turner, you will turn your badge and gun over to me now. You may either resign or be terminated, but as of right now, you are no longer a member of this police force."

Nicholas chose to resign.

After he left police headquarters, he stopped at a liquor store, and began slowly trying to drink himself dead.

Faced with no income, a savings account depleted by medical and funeral expenses, and a mind clouded completely by alcohol, Nicholas neglected the mortgage payments, and lost the house.

He turned up on his sister's doorstep with two suitcases and a cardboard box full of what few personal items he cared about. Melissa took him in, but shelter came with a price.

"Nicky, I'm worried about you," she told him, as they sat at her kitchen table. "I want my brother back. I talked to Mom and Dad, and I've talked to Marcus. Mom and Dad are very worried, and Marcus offered to slap some sense into you. You can't keep going this way. You won't get Jane and the baby back by killing yourself - they aren't coming back. All you're doing right now is hurting the rest of us."

Nicholas stared down at the table. He didn't comment, but Melissa could see that her words had an effect on him.

"Marcus made two suggestions," she continued. "With your police background, he thinks he could get you into a new security company that the government is contracted with right now - I think the name is Justice Security. He says that the man running it, Joey Justice, is a decent man and knows what he's doing.

"His other suggestion is that you work for yourself as a licensed private investigator. If you're private, Marcus said that you work only for yourself, and only on cases that you want to accept. He thinks he can send some business your way if you choose that option."

Nicholas made no sound, but tears were on his face. Melissa took his hand.

"Nicky, I love you. Whatever you choose, you can stay here with me until you can get back on your feet. But, Nicky, you've got to choose life! I don't want to lose you, and it hurts me to see you this way."

"I love you, too, 'Lis," he said. He reached for her, hugged her tight, and began crying into her hair. She hugged him back, and they stayed that way for a while.

Nicholas took a couple of days and thought about both options. He talked with Marcus, and Marcus arranged for him to meet and talk with Joey Justice. The job that Justice talked about with him was essentially an entry level job.

"But only until you show me that you can maintain yourself well enough to be trusted with more responsibility," Justice told him. "I can't really justify trusting you with a high-profile case until I'm convinced that you won't lose it under pressure. Some of our security clients require someone that can handle high levels of stress, and that are in control of themselves at all times. It's nothing personal, Mr. Turner. It's my business, and maybe my life, that I'd be trusting you with. And until you show me that you can handle it, your assignments would be extremely basic."

Nicholas liked the man, but his pride wouldn't let him accept a beginner's job, even though the salary was half again as much as he made as a cop. He wanted to be his own boss, even though the income prospects were limited to what clientele he could attract.

He became a fully-licensed private investigator. He found some office space and furnished it, with Melissa's help.

Marcus was true to his word. He helped Nicholas secure a contract with the FBI to perform non-classified background checks. Nicholas contracted with two insurance companies to investigate questionable claims. Through the next few years, he also was able to assist in several police investigations...and two of them were very high-profile cases involving missing children. Joey Justice called, and offered Nicholas a high-level position with the security company. Nicholas politely turned down Justice's offer.

He moved his offices to a larger building, and the space had a room in back that contained a full bath, a kitchen area, and a lot of space for furniture. He decided to live there rather than renting an apartment or trying to buy another house. He figured he was paying rent for the office space already, and he could save the money. The best thing to him about the new office space, although he never told Melissa or Marcus, was the frosted glass on the office door. He liked it because it made him feel like he was in a 1940s noir movie. Humphrey Bogart, look out. He paid two hundred dollars to have his name painted discreetly on the glass.

He was a success as a private investigator.

He also had weekly drinking binges.

The binges were supposed to help him forget Jane and the baby, but the reality was that they were remembering binges. Something would pop up to remind him, and that would trigger the binge. He felt as if he had a large hole in his heart that could never be filled, and the binges never made him feel better.

As time went by, however, he found that sometimes the remembering didn't cause a binge. And the binges slipped to every couple of weeks, then a couple of times a month, and, finally, just occasionally...usually when a case involved severe domestic abuse. He would never understand the mentality of people that could abuse those that loved them.

The case he had just finished involved a non-custodial spousal kidnapping. The father had kidnapped his five-year-old daughter, and fled to another state. Since crossing state lines were involved, the FBI had been called in, and Marcus was the agent in charge. When Nicholas tracked the father down, he called Marcus. But, before Marcus could arrive, the father, using the child as a shield, had accidentally shot the girl. Nicholas burst into the house, shot the father three times , and carried the wounded child to the nearest hospital. The girl lived, but it had been a very close thing.

When Nicholas arrived home the previous night, he began drinking.

But what the hell had woke him up this morning?

Nicholas looked around the room, still half-asleep. There was a little girl standing in the open doorway leading to the office area.

She was about ten, wearing jeans, a pink sleeveless pullover blouse, and tennis shoes. Her hair was brown and shoulder length, and she had blue eyes and a very cute face. She smiled at him, wiggled her fingers in a wave, and pointed out toward the office.

"Well, hi, honey," said Nicholas. "How did you get in here? What's your name?"

She didn't say anything, but only gestured again toward the office.

"Okay, honey, give me just a minute here," he said. He wiped his hand over his face, then sat up. But when he looked toward the little girl, she was gone.

"Honey?" He stood up and walked toward the office. "Where'd you go, sweetie? Where's your folks?"

When he reached the office, the little girl was not there. He looked under the desk, around the filing cabinets, even behind the ficus tree, but she was gone. He checked the office door, but it was securely locked, and the lock required a key to open or close.

"What is this happy horseshit?" he muttered to himself. The girl had simply disappeared.

He stood with his hands on his hips in the middle of the office, wondering if the drinking had finally given him the DTs, when someone knocked on the office door. It startled him so badly that he reached for the gun that was usually on his hip. He caught himself, and laughed a little. It had to be the little girl.

As he unlocked and opened the door, he said, "I wondered where you went..." He stopped, because it wasn't the little girl. It was a woman, and Nicholas thought she was one of the most attractive women he had ever seen. She was about five-five, with long blond hair and big brown eyes. She was slim, but not skinny. Her eyes were puffy, either from crying or a lack of sleep, and she had full, well-defined lips. He guessed that she was close to thirty years old.

"I'm sorry?" the woman said.

"Forgive me," he said. "Just talking to myself. Bad habit. Please come in, Ms....?"

"Richardson. Meredith Richardson." She came into the office. "I am looking for Nicholas Turner."

"That's me. Or what's left of him. Please forgive my appearance. I just finished a case last night, and I got to bed very late." He shut the door and guided the woman to the client chair beside his desk.

"Did the case involve a whiskey factory, Mr. Turner?"

He winced at the remark. "It was a tough case, and I really needed to wind down. I haven't had a chance to shower, and I apologize."

She looked into his eyes, then nodded. "Understood. You were suggested to me by an FBI agent that is acquainted with you. His name is Marcus Moore. He said that you might be...indisposed...this morning. I see that he was correct."

"Yes, ma'am. Marcus is my best friend. He knows me very well."

"Do you know who I am, Mr. Turner? Have you perhaps heard my story on the evening news, or read it in the newspaper?"

"No, I can't say that I have. I've been out of town for the last several days, and I haven't caught up on local news."

Meredith took a deep breath. "Three days ago, my daughter was walking home from a friend's house. The friend's house is three doors down from ours, in a nice neighborhood. She was kidnapped, in broad daylight, between their house and mine."

Nicholas nodded his understanding. "Go on."

"When I called the police, they issued an Amber alert, but with no real results. There were several false sightings, but nothing with real leads. I phoned the FBI last night and asked them if they could help. Agent Moore came to my home last night, and said that since the possibility exists that my daughter had crossed state lines after this length of time, the FBI would take over the case."

"Wait a minute. You called the FBI? Not the police?"

"Yes. Is that a problem?"

"No. It's just a bit unusual. Normally, in a child kidnapping, the FBI is notified immediately by the police."

Meredith shook her head. "I wouldn't know about that, Mr. Turner. I only know that I want my daughter back, and I'll ask for any help I can get. I've been an emotional wreck since she disappeared, and I felt that the police weren't doing anything to find her. Agent Moore said that you were very successful with cases like mine. He said that you had a sixth sense when it came to finding lost children. He also said that because you were private, you had an advantage that officers of the law didn't, because you didn't have to be a stickler for Constitutional rights."

"Ms. Richardson, I don't know about a sixth sense, but I have been very lucky. I've even broken a few laws in some cases. I care a great deal for children, and I feel that whatever I can do to help them is a small price to pay."

She looked down at her purse. "Mr. Turner, my daughter is only nine. She's either alone or with strangers that mean her harm. She's scared, lonely, and confused, and I'm terrified for her." A tear rolled down her cheek. "I'll pay you whatever you ask. Please help me find my daughter."

As Nicholas passed a box of tissues across the desk to her, he thought about his small visitor earlier.

"Do you have a photograph of your daughter with you?"

"Of course."

She opened her purse, pulled out a 4x6 snapshot, and passed it across the desk.

"This was taken two weeks ago when Karen and I were at the park."

The photograph showed a close-up of the little girl sitting in a swing, looking over her right shoulder at the camera. She had blond hair like her mother, with green eyes. She was very pretty, with an almost elfin face. She looked nothing like the girl that was in his office, and he was relieved. He couldn't explain it, but he hoped that his relief didn't show on his face. Right now, he needed to focus on the case and not his hallucinations.

"May I keep this?"

Meredith nodded. "Does that mean you'll help me, Mr. Turner?"

"Probably, but I have several questions, and we will need to discuss my fee."

"Money shouldn't be a problem. I'm not rich by any means, but I will be able to pay any reasonable amount."

Nicholas nodded, and took out a notebook and pen.

"Tell me about the girl's father."

"My husband died five years ago. And my daughter's name is Karen, Mr. Turner."

He smiled. "Karen it is. What was she wearing when she disappeared?"

"Jeans, a white T-shirt, and pink Reeboks. She had a blue hoodie, too."

He made notes. "What time was the disappearance?"

"Between three and three-thirty Saturday afternoon."

"Were you at home or at work?"

"I'm a moderately successful artist, and I work at home."

"What kind of artist?"

"I paint, and I contract with advertising agencies to provide artwork for commercial advertisements. I also paint portraits for individual clients, and I paint various subjects for my own pleasure."

"Do you meet with clients at your home, or do you meet with them elsewhere?"

"Both."

"Then I'll need a list of your clients going back at least a year."

"Why would you need that?"

"Right now, Ms. Richardson, everyone is a suspect. Your daughter could have been kidnapped by a current or former client, either for money or for other purposes."

"Are you implying that one of my clients might be a pedophile?"

"I don't know. The possibility is there, because the world is full of sick people. I realize that the chances of the kidnapper being one of your clients is slim, but I can't dismiss the possibility. I'm coming into this situation cold, and after three days. I've got to consider every possibility. That's going to include very intrusive questions, both for you and for people that you know, either professionally or personally. There's simply no other way to investigate a case like this. I would rather step on a few toes than run the risk of harm to that child. I hope you understand, because I can't investigate any other way."

She thought about this for a moment. "You're right, of course. I'll have the list for you this afternoon. Please forgive me, Mr. Turner. I'm not thinking right now."

Nicholas smiled at her. "You're holding up better than most of my clients, Ms. Richardson. I appreciate your strength, because it will be a great help to me." He looked down at his notebook. "Okay, back to the questions. How about boyfriends? Do you have one?"

"No. I haven't dated in some time - well over a year. Men tend to lose interest when they find out you have a child."

"Not all of us. How about social contacts? Friends, acquaintances?"

"I have two close friends, and both are women. They've been very supportive. Other than them, I don't socialize at all. I find that I don't have the time. Being a single mother is much more time-consuming than most people realize."

"I understand. I'll read the police reports later on, of course, but did any of your neighbors notice anything when your daughter disappeared?"

"No, nothing. Our neighborhood is very peaceful. Most of us have lived there for years, and we have police patrolling the area fairly regularly."

Nicholas looked over his notes. "Well, that's about all the questions I have for now." He opened a desk drawer and took out some papers. "This is a standard contract for my services. I charge two hundred and fifty dollars a day, plus expenses. Once I take a case, I investigate it my own way, and I report to you when I have something to report. I don't tolerate clients interfering with an investigation. I have resigned from investigations because of client interference, because in child cases such as this, I will perform my services always with the best interests of the child first. That doesn't always make a client happy, because I don't care who I make uncomfortable or who I piss off. Of course, if that isn't acceptable to a client, they can also dismiss me, and I will submit a bill for the time I've put in on the case. I also require a limited power of attorney from a client, giving me the power to make decisions for the child's protection. I do that for the same reason, because often decisions must be made that are difficult for a parent to choose. Also, it gives me the right to make decisions for medical services if the child should need it. Because many cases move quickly, this, unfortunately, is necessary should the child be injured." His thoughts turned briefly to his previous case. "It happens more often than I'd like. That's one of the more disturbing qualities of my work." He paused. "This power of attorney basically gives me temporary custody of Karen, Ms. Richardson, until the resolution of the case. That means that the police will have to include me in all facets of the investigation. Sometimes, the police resent what they call interference by a private investigator. With this document in hand, they might not like it, but they have no choice. Do you have any questions?"

Meredith read over the contract and the power of attorney, then looked at him.

"You're very serious about your work, aren't you?"

He nodded. "Extremely serious. I think that children are this world's most precious commodity, and I always put their interests first."

She looked into his eyes, and felt reassured and confident. "Mr. Turner, if you'll fill in the blanks on these forms, I'll sign them now."

He could feel her gaze on him as he wrote, and wondered at the fact that he was enjoying it. He wished he looked better than he did, because he felt that he looked like a street derelict. His new client was a strong, intelligent woman...and that made him think of Janey. But in a good way.

Once Meredith had signed the forms, he gave her copies, and walked her to the door.

"I'll clean myself up a little, Ms. Richardson, and then I'll come to your home. I'll need that client list, and I'll want to talk with Marcus. But, I'll get started right away on finding Karen."

"I'll have it ready, Mr. Turner. And the police have set up inside my home, so you should be able to talk with them when you arrive." She turned and looked up at him at the door. "Please find her. She's my life."

"I will do my very best. I promise you that."

She turned to leave.

"One last question, Ms. Richardson. Did you come here alone?"

She gave him an odd look. "Yes. Why?"

He shook his head. "No reason. I'll see you this afternoon."

She nodded and left, and Nicholas closed the office door behind her.

As he walked back to the bathroom to clean up, he found himself wondering about his small visitor this morning. It was odd that something woke him up just in time to meet with Meredith. Had he not awakened when he did, he might never have heard her knock. Did he really see a child in the office, or was he finally cracking up?

He decided that he didn't really care.

Chapter 2

NICHOLAS STILL COULDN'T get the little girl from his office out of his mind. As he drove to Meredith's address, he thought about what he had seen. It seemed as if she were telling him to get to the office...that Meredith was coming. But if that were the case, where did she go? She didn't come with Meredith, and she wasn't anywhere in the office...

Let it go, Nicholas, he told himself. *You're here.*

He turned into Meredith's street. She had been right - the street was in a quiet, mostly upscale neighborhood. It wasn't a rich neighborhood, but incomes would be close to six figures.

He drove past the house that Karen had visited on the day she disappeared, and paid close attention to the distance between that house and the Richardson home. There were a couple of stately old maple trees that someone could hide behind, but where would they park a getaway car? There was not a cross street, and someone would have noticed a car speeding through to the corner.

He pulled into Meredith's driveway and parked the car. Looking around, he could see what had to be Meredith's car, a small hybrid. He could see the bumper of another car parked on the grass in the backyard - that would be either Marcus or the police officers, parking so that they wouldn't be seen from the street in case the kidnappers were watching. There was a weeping willow in the front yard, and a concrete path from the driveway to the front porch. On the porch was a girl's bicycle, with pink streamers hanging from the handlebars, and a banana seat. He marveled at that - he didn't realize that banana seats were still available. He knocked on the front door.

Marcus answered the door. He looked almost as rough as Nicholas had earlier, but his off-the-rack suit was still snappy and unwrinkled. They shook hands.

"It's about time you got here, buddy-boy," said Marcus. "I've got a couple of quick things to tell you before we go inside. There won't be any fallout from last night's shooting of the little girl's father - I cleared all of that up with the local bubble-gum police department. The other thing is that the little girl will be going home this Friday."

"That's great news! How's the mother handling the whole thing?"

"As if you were the Archangel Michael riding in for battle. I think you'll get no problems collecting your fee."

"Thanks for that, Marcus. And thanks for steering Meredith to me. I just hope I have some good luck with this one."

"Well, if anyone can, it will be you."

"Hey, I had something weird happen this morning. I'd like to talk to you about it later, if you've got the time."

"Sure thing. Now come meet the cops in charge."

The two men went into Meredith's foyer. It was furnished nicely, with a genuine hall tree just inside the door. The living room was to the left. It, too, was furnished nicely but comfortably. It was a room meant to be lived in. To the right was a library, with books on floor-to-ceiling shelves, and a baby grand piano in the center of the room. Further down on the left was Meredith's studio. Nicholas caught glimpses of paintings on canvases, and what he could see were very good. Across from the studio were the stairs leading to the second floor, and at the end of the foyer was the kitchen and dining area.

The police officers had set up a field office in the dining area. Three men were seated at the spacious dining table. Electronic equipment was scattered throughout. Three men were seated at the table. One man was an officer that Nicholas knew by sight from his police department days, but the man's name eluded him for a moment. The other two were civilian techs that worked with the department that Nicholas had worked with before.

"Nicholas Turner, I'd like you to meet Detective George Parker. He has been in charge of the case from the beginning," said Marcus.

Nicholas shook hands with the officer. "Nice to meet you, Parker. I remember seeing you around the department when I worked there."

"Same here, Turner. Good to see you."

"And you already know the techs," said Marcus.

"I sure do. Mickey Hickerson and Ronnie Latimer. How're you guys?" said Nicholas.

Pleasantries were exchanged.

"Okay, guys, here's what I need to get up to speed," said Nicholas. "I need the complete file on the case, along with lists and transcripts of people that have already been talked to."

"We have that here," said Parker, with a slight disdain. "You'll have access."

"I also need a rundown on what is being done right now."

Marcus said, "We have a full technical setup, Nicky. Ms. Richardson has two land-lines coming into the house, and we have taps and tracing equipment attached to both. We also have tracing and triangulation equipment in place should she receive a call on her cell phone. Did she mention that the kidnappers had called?"

"No, she didn't. When did this happen?"

"That happened on the first day," said Marcus. "The call came in before the equipment was fully installed here, but the phone company was able to give a location anyway. It was made from a pay phone down by the docks. Of course, nobody saw anything...as usual."

"What did they say when they called?" Nicholas asked Parker.

"It's all in the file."

Nicholas looked at Marcus.

"They said that the girl was fine, and that they would be calling with instructions," replied Marcus.

"Parker, how soon did you arrive after Ms. Richardson's call to the department?" asked Nicholas.

"It's all in the file, Turner. Have at it."

Nicholas moved to face the detective, and asked very quietly, "Detective Parker, do you have a problem with me?"

"Now that you mention it, I do," said Parker. "Ten years ago, you got clean away with almost beating a subdued and unarmed suspect to death, which I think was because you're a drunk. The only reason you're here is because the fucking FBI has taken over what should have been a local case, and your ass-buddy here insists that we treat you like you were still a cop. Sure, you've lucked out on a few high-profile cases that you wormed your way into for a fee, but I think you're still a drunk! A washed-out, washed-up asshole that needs the fucking Feds to run interference for him!"

"No, Detective Parker. Mr. Turner does not need the FBI to run interference for him," said Meredith as she came into the room. "He has me for that. I can assure you that he has not 'wormed his way' into my daughter's kidnapping. I can also assure you that from what I've seen, Mr. Turner is as far from being an asshole as you are from being a competent police officer. If you had done your job properly from the beginning, Mr. Turner's presence would not be required." She turned to Marcus. "A question, Agent Moore: Is it proper procedure for the police to immediately notify the FBI in cases of child abduction?"

"Normally, yes, Ms. Richardson."

She turned again to Parker. "Can you offer a valid reason explaining why that didn't happen, Detective Parker? Is guarding your 'pissing grounds' more important than the life of a nine-year-old girl?"

Parker looked subdued and stammered, "Well, no ma'am...but, see, it's like this..."

"No, Detective Parker. Your incompetence has seriously jeopardized the retrieval and safety of my daughter. This is something that your bluster and chest-thumping will neither change nor silence." She turned again to Marcus. "Am I correct in assuming that you are now in charge of this investigation, Agent Moore?"

"Yes, ma'am. The Bureau has taken full control of the case."

"In your opinion, is Mr. Turner my best hope of safely finding my daughter and bringing her home to me?"

"With the Bureau's full assistance and leadership, yes. I firmly believe that."

She turned to Parker. "Detective Parker, your services are no longer wanted or required. I want you to leave my home immediately. I will ask Agent Moore to meet with the Chief of Police to discuss your conduct, and I will support any investigation into your performance here."

"But, Ms. Richardson..."

"Now, Detective Parker."

Parker looked at Marcus, then at Nicholas. "This isn't over yet, asshole. You still have to work in this city, and I look forward to busting your ass."

Nicholas looked into Parker's eyes. "And I will look back on it, Parker."

"Is that a threat? Are you actually threatening a police officer?"

Nicholas smiled at him.

"Leave *now*, Detective Parker, or I will have you charged with criminal trespass," said Meredith.

Without another word, Parker stormed through the foyer and slammed the front door as he left.

The two technicians were staring at both Nicholas and Meredith with their mouths hanging open.

"Gentlemen, please close your mouths. You look like cousins from the Ozark Mountains," said Meredith.

They closed their mouths with a snap.

Meredith turned to Marcus and Nicholas. "Gentlemen, since I have alienated the local police department, please don't turn me into a liar. Find my daughter, and find her quickly."

Marcus nodded at her. Nicholas looked at her with admiration, then nodded. Her strength continued to impress him.

As she left the room, Marcus mumbled to Nicholas, "Now, that woman is a keeper, Nicky!"

He didn't say so out loud, but Nicholas agreed.

He sat at Meredith's dining table and read through the case file. Interviews had been conducted with all of the neighbors on the street, and on the streets on both sides. No one had seen anything unusual. Interviews had also been conducted with Meredith's friends, and several of her current clients. Family members had been contacted by phone, since Meredith had no family living in the city.

The transcript of the phone call was indeed in the file. He read through it, and discovered nothing that Marcus hadn't told him. The phone company had traced the call to the pay phone beside Kenzie's Seafood, a restaurant at the docks noted for its good food. The police had talked to people at the restaurant, but it was a popular public place, with lots of people coming and going. No one had seen anything unusual.

Nicholas closed the case file. He wondered where he could start now, since the police had already interviewed everyone he could think to talk to, and had come up with nothing. He shook his head. You could say what you would about Parker's personality, but he had been pretty thorough.

It was as if the girl had disappeared into thin air.

Just like his morning visitor.

Marcus came in and sat down beside him. "Anything?"

Nicholas shook his head. "No. Looks like the bases have all been covered."

"I'm going to have two agents assigned to this case. I'll be sending them out to talk to everyone again, although I think it's going to be a dead end. Truthfully, Nicky, right now all we can do is wait for the kidnappers to call again."

"We're missing something, Marcus. We have to be. And it's something that's so obvious that we're not thinking about it."

"Do you think it's the mother?"

Nicholas shook his head. "No, I don't think so. For all the strength she's shown, I think she's about to fall apart."

"It's been done before."

"Not this time."

Marcus looked at his friend. "Getting a little defensive about the lady, Nicky?"

Nicholas said nothing.

"Of course, I couldn't blame you," said Marcus. "She's a very attractive woman."

"Shut up, Marcus."

"All I'm saying is that Janey's been gone for ten years, Nicky. I think it would be very healthy for you to show an interest in another woman. Jane would not have wanted you to be alone."

"Let it alone, Marcus."

"Whatever you say, my friend." He gestured toward the case file. "Do you have any ideas at all? Can you think of anything?"

"I might try to track down an informer or two. Maybe if I get the word out, someone will come up with something I can use to get started."

"Sounds good. I think I'm going to try to get a few hours' sleep. Maybe if I lose myself in dreamland, somebody there will tell me what to do."

The comment made Nicholas remember his visitor. He told Marcus about it.

"Interesting. She disappeared?"

"Completely."

"I arrested this guy once for bank robbery. He swore that he did it because a goblin had told him to. He described the goblin with great detail, and said that it was standing right next to him, laughing."

"Thanks, buddy. That makes me feel so much better."

"Maybe you were dreaming."

"Then how did I wind up standing in front of the office door when Meredith showed up?"

"Sleepwalking and coincidence."

Nicholas thought about that. "Maybe. But it seemed so real, Marcus."

"I don't have an answer, Nicky. It could have been a dream, maybe triggered by shooting that little girl's father last night."

"Maybe."

"Or you've got a rabbit hole in your office, and the girl's name is Alice."

Nicholas laughed at his friend. "Marcus, you are such a horse's ass."

"I'm a sleepy horse's ass. At least you had some sleep last night." He stood up. "I think I'm going to leave the techs here and go crash. If you need me, call my cell."

Nicholas waved an okay, and looked for Meredith. She was in the back yard, sitting in a swing on a large children's swing set. As he watched her from the back door window, he realized that she really was an attractive woman. He went outside to talk to her.

She was staring at the ground as he approached. She looked much like a lost little girl herself. Although he had seen this kind of empty feeling in mothers before, this time his heart wrenched a little. She spoke to him as he got closer.

"What do you think she's feeling right now, Mr. Turner?"

"Honestly? I have no way of knowing. I wish I did."

"I think she's scared. I think she's wondering why Mommy isn't coming to get her. I think she's feeling that her Mommy doesn't want her any more."

"I'm sure she isn't feeling that way, Ms. Richardson. She knows her mother loves her."

"I wish I could reassure her of that, Mr. Turner. I'd give anything to just hold her again."

"You'll hold her again. I promise you that. And will you please call me Nicholas?"

She nodded. "If you will call me Meredith."

"Done."

"So, what's next, Nicholas? Do you have any ideas?"

"I have some informants that my have heard something. I came out here to tell you that I'm going now to find them. It's almost dark, so they'll be coming out. They're not the best people in the world, but they have their uses."

Impulsively, he took her hand. "I'll find her, Meredith."

"I know. But will it be in time?"

He had no answer.

Chapter 3

NICHOLAS WAS DRIVING along Hooker Hollow. The street's real name was Third Street, but because of the bars, adult stores, and peep shows, the street had earned its new name before he ever joined the police department. Although it was just after nightfall, it was still early for most of the Hollow's regulars to begin the evening's business. There were a few hookers shouting at passing vehicles, but their shouts didn't have the exuberance that would be exhibited later. There were a few people walking along the street, some strutting as if they owned the city, and some being furtive, as if they were afraid that their grandmothers would catch them there.

He had decided that his best bet among his informers would be Snickers. Snickers was a former junkie that had been involved in almost every kind of crime to feed his habit. As a street patrolman, Nicholas had arrested Snickers for robbing a liquor store. Snickers immediately began offering information about anything Nicholas wanted to know, as long as Nicholas didn't lock him up. Nicholas made a counter offer: if the information turned out to be accurate, he would make the charges go away.

The information was accurate, and Nicholas was true to his word. Their give and take relationship grew, and information from Snickers was directly responsible for Nicholas's promotion to Detective. As a gift, Nicholas paid for Snickers to enter a good rehab clinic to clean himself up.

A grateful Snickers still kept in touch with his underground connections, but he remained clean. He had a knack for computers, and held a job as a computer programmer. He was a small, ratty-looking man, and still had the nervous twitches that he had developed as a junkie. He hung out most nights at McFeely's, a bar in the Hollow. McFeely's, commonly known on the street as "McFeelme's", was a tough place that served hard drinks to harder customers, and had a reputation of being able to provide almost anything that a person might be looking for. Fights broke out there regularly, but rarely involved Snickers.

Nicholas parked on the street a block and a half away from McFeely's. As he got out of the car, a woman approached him.

"Nicky Turner! Nicky, when are you gonna stop all this *fore*-play and fuck my brains out, baby?" she said.

"Tiffany, you'd kill me," he said playfully. "I'm not about to pay to have myself killed."

"Now that's just *cold*," she replied. "I heard that you was fuckin' *Jas*-mine, and I'm a whole lot better than her."

"Not true, Tiff. You know you're my only lover. Besides, I wouldn't fuck Jasmine with a stolen dick and someone else pushing."

Tiffany laughed. "I heard *that*!"

"Have you seen Snickers tonight?"

"Naw, but I ain't been lookin' for his narrow ass, either."

"If you see him, would you tell him to meet me at McFeelme's?"

"Sho will, baby."

"Take care, Tiff."

"You too, ya big stud!"

Nicholas began walking toward McFeely's, nodding to some of the people he knew. Word had circulated in the last ten years about the kind of work that Nicholas did since he became a private investigator. A full ninety percent of his cases involved children to some degree, and, among criminals, the people that messed with children were the lowest of the low. If Nicholas were on a child abuse case, he could count on help from practically everyone in the hollow, whereas a child support case might not get him any help at all. This criminal hierarchy constantly surprised him, but he took his help where he could get it.

He was a block away from McFeely's when he noticed the little girl.

She was standing in front of McFeely's staring intensely at Nicholas. When she noticed that he'd seen her, she waved a "come on, hurry up" wave at him with one hand, while pointing to the bar with the other. It was the same little girl that he had seen in his office that morning, and she was still dressed as she was then.

He froze for a minute in the middle of the sidewalk. One of the people passing by touched him on the shoulder and asked, "Hey, you all right, man?"

"I don't know," Nicholas replied. "Hey! Stay right there!" He started running toward the bar, pointing at the little girl. "Don't move!"

People were turning around to see who Nicholas was talking to. As Nicholas drew closer to the little girl, she smiled at him and gave him another little finger wave. Just before he reached her, a group of people came out of McFeely's and blocked her from view. When they moved, the girl was gone. He looked all around, but there was nowhere that she could be hiding. There were no alleys to duck into, and no cars to hide inside. She had disappeared into thin air.

Unless she had gone into the bar.

He walked inside the bar just in time to see a huge man connect his fist to the side of Snickers' head. Snickers fell into the booths along the wall, stunned. The huge man reached into his jacket pocket and pulled a knife. He advanced toward Snickers.

Nicholas didn't hesitate. He ran to the man and gave him two quick kidney punches, left and right. The man turned slowly around toward him.

Oh, shit, thought Nicholas.

"I don't know you, asshole. But if you want a piece of his shit, I can definitely give it to you!"

Nicholas held up his hands in a "wait a minute" gesture, then drove the stiffened fingers of his left hand into the man's Adam's apple. The big man's eyes widened and he dropped his knife. His hands went to his throat, and he wheezed. A small trickle of blood began running from the side of his mouth. He staggered.

"You can breathe, big boy. It may hurt like hell, but you can breathe. Now get the fuck out of here," said Nicholas. The big man lumbered out of the bar.

Snickers was being attended to by Hank McFeely himself. McFeely helped Snickers to his feet. Snickers waved him away.

McFeely said to Nicholas, "Thanks, Nicky. That guy would've killed Snickers, and I didn't think my baseball bat would have stopped him."

"To tell the truth, Hank, I thought I'd bit off more than I could chew."

McFeely laughed. "Looked like it. You shoulda seen your face when the kidney punches didn't work."

Nicholas laughed too. "Hey, Hank. You didn't see a little girl come in here just before Snickers got punched, did you?"

"Nope, but I didn't see *you* come in, either. I'll ask around."

"Thanks, Hank."

Nicholas took Snickers' arm to steady him. "Why did that mountain hit you, Snick?"

Snickers shook his head. "He told me to get out of his way, ya know?"

"What did you say to him?"

"I told him to go fuck a tree - it'd be better than his wife."

Nicholas started laughing, and, after a minute, so did Snickers.

"Pretty stupid, huh, Nicky?"

"Yep. Come on, Sugar Ray, I got questions for you."

They went to a booth in the back and sat down. Hazel, the waitress, brought them each a beer.

"Compliments of Hank, boys. Drink up."

"Thank you, Hazel," said Nicholas.

Snickers took a long pull from his beer. "So whatcha got goin', Nicky? Looks like I owe ya one, ya know?"

McFeely came to the booth before Nicholas could answer. "No little girl, Nicky. Are you sure she came in here?"

"No, Hank, I'm not. But thank you for asking around, and thanks for the beers."

"My pleasure, fellas." He went away.

Nicholas said, "Three days ago, in the middle of the afternoon, a little girl was kidnapped." He told the story.

"I got nothin', Nicky, but I'll keep my ears open for ya." Snickers tapped his lips with the tip of his index finger. "I *have* heard a rumor or two about something, but I dunno if it has anything to do with this or not, ya know?"

"What?"

"Well, there's this buncha rich guys got 'em a little group, see? I don't mean they're here in the city - they're all over the world. But they like to have kinda weird sex, and they don't like hookers. They want 'em fresh, ya know?"

"Go on."

"Buddy of mine got contacted a couple of years ago. The guy said that this group would pay a guy to kidnap a woman, but she had to be a certain type of lady...kind of a 'made to order' type thing, ya know? Say a lady with brown hair and certain measurements...no older than twenty-one." Snickers drank beer. "I guess these guys would like pass her around till they're all done fuckin' her out, then they get rid of her."

"Get rid of her how, Snick?"

Snickers folded his hand into a gun shape and pointed it at his own head. "So I'm wonderin', Nicky, if maybe these guys have decided to go to a short-eyes thing, ya know?"

"Did your buddy take the contract?"

Snickers shook his head. "Naw, that shit brings the Feds down on ya like stink on shit, ya know? He didn't want to go to the big joint so some rich fat guys could get their rocks off."

"How was your buddy supposed to notify them when the job was done?"

"I dunno for sure, Nicky. It didn't get that far for him, ya know? But he got the idea that the contact guy was some big mucky-muck that couldn't be touched. Nothin' was said, but that's the idea he got."

"Think you could get in touch with him tonight?"

"I can only try, ya know? But I'll call ya if I get something."

"Listen, Snick, you've heard me talk about Marcus Moore, right?"

"The Fed? Yeah, I remember."

"He knows who you are and what we do, so if you can't get hold of me for some reason, you call him." Nicholas took out a small memo pad, wrote down Marcus's cell phone number, and gave it to Snickers.

"Must be a hot case for ya, huh, Nicky?"

"No, it's a cold case...but I think with your help we can solve it. I need anything you can get as soon as you get it."

"I know, I know...ya need it yesterday."

"And do me another favor, Snickers."

"What's that, Nicky?"

"Next time, look at a guy before you mouth off at him."

Nicholas left the bar while Snickers laughed.

Chapter 4

OUTSIDE THE BAR, NICHOLAS looked around again, trying to figure out where the little girl could have hidden herself. No place that he could see would have been able to hide her that quickly. Shaking his head, he walked back to his car.

There was a parking ticket under the windshield.

He looked around. As far as he could tell, he was parked legally. No fire hydrants, no "no parking" or "parking between the hours of" signs anywhere, and he wasn't blocking any delivery areas.

Parker, he thought. The detective had decided to be petty, and had obviously instructed the street patrolmen to harass him wherever they found his car. Well, that was a problem that could be dealt with right away.

When Nicholas had resigned from the department, the Chief of Detectives told him that if he wanted to pull himself together, the chief would do anything within reason to help him. The chief had kept his word, and had even sent some business to Nicholas. He had turned out to be a friend.

Now, the former Chief of Detectives was Chief of the city's entire police department.

Nicholas took out his cell phone and dialed the Chief's home number.

"Hello?"

"Hi, Chief! This is Nicholas Turner."

"Nicholas! How's it going? I heard that you solved another one last night. How many times are you planning to be a hero, Turner?"

"I'm no hero, sir. I'm just lucky, I guess."

"I hear that you're looking into the Richardson kidnapping."

"Yes, sir, that's correct."

"I heard from the Richardson woman. I also heard from that FBI friend of yours. Both of them told me that Parker gave you some grief. I called him onto the carpet this afternoon, read him the riot act."

Nicholas smiled. "I'm sure you did, sir. That's why I'm calling. I think Parker's decided to harass me." He told the Chief about the parking ticket.

"Who wrote that ticket, Turner?"

Nicholas looked at the ticket. The neon brightness of the Hollow gave him plenty of light. "It looks like Patrolman Martin, Chief."

"Do me a favor, Nicholas. Can you stay put for about fifteen minutes?"

"Sure."

"Thanks, son. And if there's anything you need from me, you call me. Anytime."

"Thank you, Chief." Nicholas hung up and leaned against his car.

Tiffany apparently had scored some business, because she wasn't around. But several other Hollow regulars stopped to talk to him. They asked how he was and what he was working on. When he told them, everyone offered to help, and promised to call him if they heard anything. Again, the sentiment among the criminal element amazed him. Some of these people would kill you for your shoes, but if a kid was in trouble, they rallied around to help.

He had been leaning against his car for about ten minutes when a city police patrol car double parked on the other side of his car. The regulars that had been talking to him scattered. Both officers got out of the car and came over to him.

"Mr. Turner?" asked one of the officers.

"That's me."

"Sir, I'm Patrolman Jason Martin. I believe I mistakenly issued you a parking citation. If you would give it back to me, I'll take care of it, sir, with my apologies."

"Thanks, Martin. Can you give Detective Parker a message for me?"

"Yes, sir."

"Tell him to back off from me while he still has a job. Tell him I'll fuck up his life if he doesn't."

"I'll be happy to pass that along, sir. Sorry for any inconvenience."

"Good night, gentlemen," said Turner.

As he drove away, he thought about Parker. He knew that asking the patrolman to pass along that particular message would only enrage the detective into escalating the harassment, but he didn't care. Something about the detective rubbed him the wrong way, but he couldn't put a finger on what bothered him.

His thoughts turned to the little girl again as he drove to his office. She had shown up twice now, and the second time he was stone sober, so that made the idea of a hallucination less likely. Both times had been just before something happened. The second time had been barely in time to keep Snickers from being cut or stabbed, or maybe even killed. And the first time had been just before Meredith's arrival at the office. So, no, the girl had not been a hallucination. But who was she? And where the hell had she disappeared to?

He pulled into a McDonald's drive-thru and ordered a burger and fries. After he received his food, he drove the rest of the way to his office. He climbed the stairs, unlocked the door, and went inside. The mail was on the floor in front of the door. He picked it up and sat down behind his desk. He had a message on his answering machine. He pressed "play" for his message, then pressed the power button on his computer. He needed to type up everything that had happened that day in the current case, as well as the final report from the case he wrapped up last night. The message was from the mother in his previous case.

"Mr. Turner, there aren't any words that can make you understand how grateful I am to you. Jessica is doing fine, and can come home on Friday. I would be honored if you would come to the house to meet her..." Nicholas stopped the message playback. He was embarrassed by the attention, and her gushing thanks made him feel uncomfortable. Also, he didn't really think that the girl would want to meet the man who killed her father. He would submit his final report along with his bill to the mother, and be done with it.

He called up the word processing program that he used for his reports, and typed out the final report. He then opened his billing software and prepared the bill. He printed both, put them in an envelope, and prepared it for mailing. He entered Meredith's billing information into the billing program and listed the amount of the retainer she had paid him, then closed the program. On the word processing program, he opened a blank page and began thinking about what he wanted to say in his notes.

His sandwich and fries remained uneaten - he had forgotten them. The refrigerator in his living area was almost empty, so he decided to go downstairs to the soft drink machine just outside for something to drink. He took his letter with him to drop into the mailbox.

When he returned, he opened his dinner and took a big bite from the sandwich. Chewing, he turned to the computer.

"hi" was on the screen.

Shaking his head and thinking that he must have hit a couple of keys, he cleared the word. Before he could do anything else, "hi" appeared again. He leaned back in his chair, looking at the screen. The word appeared again under the first one, then again, looking like:

hi

hi

hi

Nicholas erased the words with the backspace button.

They appeared again, the same as previously.

hi

hi

hi

"What the hell is this?" he mumbled to himself.

As he reached for the backspace key again, the screen came alive.

"hihihihihihihihihihihihihihi..." appeared, continuing over the entire screen. Nicholas, astounded, quickly pressed the "Escape" key. The word stopped.

He leaned back in his chair, watching the computer screen. Getting an idea, he disconnected the Internet connection and leaned back in his chair again.

A new word appeared on the screen as he watched. "hello," it read.

Goosebumps rose along his arms. After a moment, he reached for the keyboard and typed.

"is somebody there?" he typed.

Almost before he finished the question, "yes" appeared.

"who are you?"

"you"

"what is your name?"

"cant tell you"

"what do people call you?"

"nothing"

"what are you doing?"

"talking to you"

"why don't you talk to me in my office?"

"did that already"

"when?"

"this morning"

"are you meredith?"

"no"

He leaned back in his chair again and thought for a minute. The only other person that had been in his office that morning was the little girl. He began typing again.

"are you the little girl?"

"yes"

"who are you?"

"you"

"you can't be me. I'm not a little girl"

"you"

He thought for a minute, then typed.

"how did you disappear from my office so quickly?"

"went away"

"how?"

"went away"

"did you wake me up this morning?"

"yes"

"why?"

"you had to get up"

"why?"

"you had to meet the woman"

"do you mean meredith?"

"yes"

"why?"

"you had to meet her"

"why did i have to meet her?"

"you have to save karen"

"what do you know about karen?"

"cant tell you"

"why not?"

"im not allowed"

"not allowed?"

"im not allowed i can only help you"

"telling me what you know would help me."

"i can only help you you have to be the one to find her"

"how are you doing this?"

"doing what"

"making words appear on this screen"

"dont know just thinking"

"why don't you come back to my office and talk to me?"

"cant talk yet"

"can't talk yet? aren't you allowed?"

"not yet"

Nicholas stopped typing for a moment to give himself time to think. He was confused, because the conversation was a big riddle. In his mind, he wasn't convinced that he was conversing with the little girl. But, if it wasn't her, who was this? And what did she...or whoever...mean by some of these answers?

He had a way to find out for sure if it was the little girl.

He typed, "have i seen you since this morning?"

"yes"

"where?"

"hollow"

Nicholas was now convinced that it was the little girl, because he hadn't had a chance to mention seeing her again to anyone. He didn't know how she could be talking to him on the computer, in a word processing program with no outside connection...and yet, here it was. That gave him another batch of questions.

"why did you come to the hollow?"

"you had to save snickers"

"why?"

"he can help you"

"help me with what?"

"finding karen"

"how did you know that snickers needed help?"

"just knew"

"did someone tell you that he was in trouble?"

"kinda just knew"

More riddles. Nicholas decided that he had to find the girl and talk to her, so he tried something else.

"where are you?"

"with you"

"i don't see you here. Where are you?"

"with you im always with you"

"please don't lie. i can protect you, if you're afraid."

"not afraid"

"then where are you?"

"with you"

"who are you?"

"you im part of you"

"are you saying that i'm typing both sides of our talk?"

"no"

"then who are you?"

"you im part of you"

Goosebumps started rising along his arms again. Nicholas was confused. Someone must have rigged his computer while he had been gone, but he couldn't figure out how. But no one knew that he had seen the little girl again tonight. He couldn't help but think that maybe he was losing his mind, and that he was typing both sides of the conversation without knowing it. He decided to try something else.

He typed, "is karen okay?" then put his hands under his legs.

"yes shes scared hungry" appeared on the screen.

He took his hands out from under his legs. If he typed that last line, he had deluded himself into thinking that his hands were under his legs. He didn't think that was true, but how could he be sure?

He typed, "where is karen?"

"i can only help you you have to be the one to find her" appeared again on the screen.

"telling me where she is will help me. will you tell me?"

"cant not allowed"

"Dammit," he said under his breath.

"dont do that" appeared.

He was surprised. "don't do what?" he typed.

"swear"

"can you hear me?"

"yes"

"do you have a microphone hidden here?"

"no"

"then how did you hear me?"

"just did"

"where are you?" he typed again.

"with you silly i told you"

"if you're here, show me."

"cant"

"why can't you?"

"snickers"

A knock sounded on the glass of his office door. Nicholas was startled so badly, he drew his gun. "Come in!" he called out, aiming his gun at the door.

It opened, and Snickers walked in. He saw the Nicholas aiming the gun at him, threw his hands up, and said, "JEEZ, Nicky, it's ME!"

Nicholas put his gun back in its holster, and shook his head. "Sorry, Snickers. You startled me."

"Jeez, Nicky, ya gonna shoot everybody that comes through the door? What's wrong with ya?"

"Nothing, buddy. Just some weird things happening with this case."

"Ya gotta be careful, ya know? How would it be with ya savin' my bacon earlier, then shootin' me yerself? 'Specially when I got news, ya know?"

Nicholas quickly put his finger to his lips in a "shh" gesture, then held his hand up like a traffic cop. He got up from behind the desk, took Snickers by the arm, and said, "Come on, let's take a walk."

In the hallway, Nicholas locked the office door, then quickly steered Snickers downstairs and outside.

"Snick, did you tell anybody that you were coming here? I mean anybody!"

"No, Nicky, I just drove over when I got some news, ya know? Why, somebody after me?" he said, looking around the parking lot.

"No, but something screwy is going on here, and I can't figure it out."

"Well, lemme tell ya what I got, and then I'm gonna go lay low till ya figure it out, ya know? I don't think I wanna get in the middle of somethin' that might not be in my best interest, ya know?"

"I don't blame you, Snick. Did you talk to your guy?"

"Yeah. Like I said earlier, he turned it down, ya know? But he knows the guy that took the job. And the guy that took the job might talk to ya, accordin' to my guy."

"That's great, Snickers! Maybe it's a lead."

"I think it is, Nicky, 'cause my guy says that the goon is hidin' out, ya know? He thinks somebody's after him."

"Who's after him?"

"I dunno. My guy didn't say, and I didn't ask any questions, ya know? But my guy gave me the address where you can find the goon. He'll be lookin' for ya. I think he wants some protection, ya know?"

"I'll give it to him if he's got something I can use. Where is he?"

"Here, I wrote it down, ya know?" Snickers gave Nicholas a piece of paper with a name and an address scribbled on it. Looked like it was in the industrial park. "Not bad for a coupla phone calls, huh, Nicky?"

"Not bad at all, Snickers. Thanks, buddy."

"Hey, I just wanna help the kid, ya know? I'll see ya, Nicky. Call me if ya need anything else. And be careful, ya know?"

"You, too."

Snickers left, and Nicholas went back inside the building and climbed the stairs to his office. He unlocked the door and went inside.

The computer screen had a new line at the bottom.

"tell marcus where youre going"

Nicholas collapsed onto the chair behind the desk and stared at the screen. After a moment, he reached for the keyboard.

"how do you know i'm going anywhere?"

"saw him heard him he's funny"

"how do you know snickers?"

"just do"

Then another line appeared under that.

"he loves you you saved him he calls you his big brother"

Nicholas let that sink in for a minute.

"how can you know that?"

"just do"

"have you met snickers?"

"no"

"do you want to meet snickers?"

"yes"

"why?"

"he loves you"

"do you know marcus?" he typed.

"no"

"have you ever talked to marcus?"

"no he loves you too you do what he cant"

"how do you know that if you haven't met him?"

"just do tell him where youre going its important"

"where am i going?"

"to talk to that man"

"why should i tell marcus?"

"you have to its dangerous please tell him"

Nicholas got an idea.

"no."

"no what"

"i'm not telling marcus where i'm going."

"you have to"

"no."

"please"

"no."

"pleasepleasepleasepleasepleasepleaseplease..." began filling the screen. Nicholas hit the "Escape" key again, then began typing.

"i'll tell him on one condition."

"what"

"you say you're with me. show me."

No answer appeared on the screen. Nicholas typed again.

"show me, and i'll call marcus."

"trying watch"

Nicholas sat back in the chair, waiting. His soda can abruptly turned over, spilling soda all over the desk. He jumped up trying to keep his pants from getting wet. He took tissues from the box on his desk and mopped up the spilled mess. When he was done, he looked at the computer screen. A new sentence appeared that sent chills down his spine.

"oops i made a mess sorry"

He stared at the sentence for a moment, trying to make sense of the situation. Finally, he reached for the keyboard and typed.

"did you knock the can over?"

"yes it was hard almost couldnt"

"are you a ghost?" he typed slowly.

"no silly"

"who are you?"

"i told you i'm you part of you"

"if you're not a ghost, what are you?"

"cant tell you im not allowed yet you have to guess"

Nicholas was surprised to find that he was fascinated and curious, but not afraid. He kept feeling that if he asked the right question, he would figure out what...or who...he was dealing with, but he couldn't think of what else he could ask. He returned to a subject that they had passed over.

"earlier you said that i had to meet the woman. why?"

"youre supposed to"

"why am i supposed to?"

"youre hers shes yours youre supposed to be"

Nicholas, stunned by this remark, leaned back in his chair. The little girl was standing to his right. He jumped, and shouted, "Fuck!"

The little girl had a look of concentration on her face. Words appeared on the computer screen.

"i told you dont do that its not nice"

"Okay, sweetie, I don't know how you got in here, but you aren't leaving until I get some answers!" said Nicholas as he reached for the girl's arm.

His hand passed *through* her arm. His hand had a warm tingle. His face went through several emotions...disbelief, fear, wonder.

"How did you...how did that..." he stammered.

She had the look of concentration again, and words again appeared on the screen.

"i didnt i cant be real unless i try really hard its dangerous"

He looked at the girl, and for the first time, studied her features. The resemblance to his dead wife was very strong.

"Janey?" he said slowly. The girl shook her head, and a word appeared on the screen.

"no"

Then he remembered something that he had tried so hard to forget. The night that his life went straight down the path to Hell.

He never told Jane, but their miscarried child had been a girl.

Their daughter.

With tears bubbling up into his eyes, he stammered, "Muh...Madeline?"

The girl nodded, then said, "Hi, Daddy."

Nicholas did something then that he had never done in his thirty-six years. He fainted.

Chapter 5

NICHOLAS WAS DREAMING.

In his dream, he and Jane were on a picnic in a park. Their daughter, Madeline, was running and playing while they put the food on the blanket. Jane called Madeline to come and eat, and they had one of their best meals ever.

After they had eaten, they packed everything back into the basket. Madeline was playing again, and Nicholas was lying on the blanket with his head in Jane's lap. Jane was stroking his hair, and they were both watching Madeline play.

"She loves you so very much, Nicky," said Jane.

He nodded.

"You've been given a great gift, you big stud," she said. "She's argued all this time that you were so cheated, and that it wasn't fair for you to be lonely, especially since you were helping so many children."

"I'm just doing what comes naturally, Janey," he said. "I love kids...always have."

"It isn't just because of the kids, Nicky. It's because you always do the right thing...but, this time you're going to need a lot of help to find that little girl before it's too late. Plus, it's probably the only way to shut Madeline up," she said with a smile. "So, you've got her for a while, and neither of us knows for how long. But, there are restrictions on her, and she'll tell you what they are. Listen to her, Nicky. She'll point you in the direction that you need to go."

He nodded again, growing increasingly sleepier.

"I love you, Nicholas Turner, and I want you to be happy again." She kissed his forehead, and as he finally drifted off to sleep, he heard her murmur, "I want you to move on, stud. It's okay. And love our angel, will you?"

As he drifted off to sleep, he heard Madeline saying, "Daddy, wake up. Wake up, Daddy! Wake up! "

Nicholas awoke with a start. He was leaning back in the desk chair. Wow, what a dream he had...

"Gosh, Daddy, you're such a spaz!" said Madeline.

Everything came rushing back to him. "How is this possible? You were never born, you can't be here!"

She giggled. "Daaa-aaad, didn't Mom talk to you?"

He said, "I was dreaming of her just now."

She nodded. "Yep, she talked to you. She said she would."

Nicholas tried to touch her face. His hand passed through her again.

"Stop it, Daddy, that tickles!"

"Wait a minute, Madeline. How are you suddenly able to talk? You said that you weren't allowed."

"I wasn't allowed...not till you guessed who I was. It was one of those poopy *restrictions*!" she said angrily. "You can be so *dumb* sometimes. I didn't think you'd ever guess!"

Nicholas still couldn't believe what was happening. He shook his head. How could the spirit of his daughter be standing here talking to him? It wasn't possible. She had never even been born, and yet here she was - apparently at the age and stage of development that she would be in had she lived. And she was so beautiful - the resemblance to Jane was incredible, but he could see himself in her, too.

He had a million questions, but he had no idea where to start. He finally decided to start with the basics.

"Madeline, why are you here? And why now?"

"Oh, Daddy. Didn't you listen to Mom?"

He nodded, remembering his dream.

"I'm here to help you because you need it. You need *me*. Mom said you needed cl...clo..."

"Closure?"

"Yeah, that's the word. Plus, I love you, Daddy. I'm always with you, and so is Mom. But you didn't know that, and you need to."

Nicholas nodded. He had a tear slowly running down his face, but he wasn't aware of it.

"You and your mother are all I've thought about for the last ten years. I can't help but wonder what could have been...and miss what *should* have been. And, oh *God*, it's hurt so much."

"I know. But, Daddy, you've got a second chance to be happy. I'm not sposed to tell you about that, but I don't care. You're my *daddy*."

"Madeline, how can I have a second chance? You and your mother are both dead! How will that work?"

"It isn't with us, Daddy. Our time here is over. Yours isn't. Your second chance is with Meredith and Karen. But it's only if you save Karen in time! And you won't save her in time if I don't help you. That's why I'm here, to help you." Madeline paused. "Oh, poop...I wasn't sposed to tell you that, either."

Madeline began fading gradually. As she faded from sight, she shouted, "Talk to the man, Daddy! And tell Marcus where you're going! It's import..." She faded out completely before she could finish her sentence. Nicholas tried grabbing for her, but his hands passed through where she was standing. He again felt the warm tingle.

He sat back in the chair. What did she mean by a second chance with Meredith and Karen? If she meant a second chance at love, he wasn't sure he wanted that. Meredith wasn't Jane. Granted, she was a strong woman, and was very attractive...he chased that train of thought out of his head. His grief had been his driving force for ten years, and he didn't see a reason to change that. Not even for a ghostly daughter or a dead dream wife. He still wasn't sure that he wasn't imagining the whole thing.

But, one thing was sure. He had a little girl to find, and he had a lead thanks to Snickers. He looked at his watch. Eleven o'clock. He had to go talk to the man. He put on his jacket, made sure that his gun was in its holster, and he picked up his cell phone. He stopped for a few seconds, looking at it. He decided to call Marcus. It wouldn't hurt to let somebody know where he was going...

"Marcus Moore."

"Hey, Marcus, it's me. Snickers gave me a lead, and I'm going to talk to a guy. It might not amount to anything," Nicholas said. He paused for a minute, then said, "But I've got a feeling that it may be the lead I've been looking for."

"Nicky, I'm in a meeting right now, but I've got a couple of things I want to go over with you, too. Where are you meeting your guy?"

Nicholas read off the address. "The guy's name is Richard 'Ricky' Logan. Snickers said that somebody hired this guy to kidnap a woman matching a general description. He said he thought it was for a group of rich people that wanted a specific type for some kind of sex games."

"A kidnap-to-order. The Bureau's all over that, Nicky. We've got several open cases that we think fit that scenario. Do you think the Richardson kidnapping is one of those?"

"Again, Marcus, I'm not sure of anything. But I have a strong feeling about it."

"Gotcha, buddy. I've got the address, and I'll tag along as soon as I'm done with this meeting. I'll see you there."

"Thanks, Marcus." They hung up.

"Okay, Madeline. I did what you asked me to. Now let's go see if you're right." He waited to see if there was an answer. There wasn't. He shook his head. *I'm cracking up*, he thought to himself. *This* can't *be real*. He left the office, locking the door behind him, then walked downstairs, outside, and into his car.

As he began driving toward the address, Madeline began fading back into view in the passenger seat. She was talking, and her voice faded in as she did.

"...and you can't make me!" she was saying. She crossed her arms and slumped down into the seat with a determined look on her face.

Nicholas was startled again. "Dammit, Madeline! You have *got* to start warning me when you do that!"

"Don't swear, Daddy."

"I'll swear if I want to, little lady. It doesn't matter, because there is no way you are real. You're all in my imagination."

Tears began welling in her eyes. "How can you think that, Daddy? Aren't I here? Can't you see me?"

Nicholas glanced at her. "Yes, I see you. I'm talking to you. But how do I know that you're real? How do I know that I'm not having some serious hallucinations? Hell, I can't even hug you!"

"But you can, Daddy! Look, I'll show you!" she said.

He kept glancing at her. She closed her eyes, and a look of fierce concentration appeared on her face. He saw a bright white glow gradually surround her, then it began to slowly fade. With her eyes still closed, she slowly reached out with her right hand and squeezed his hand.

Nicholas, surprised, jerked his hand away and swerved into the left lane. Bringing the car back under control, he pulled over to the side of the street and parked. He had actually felt her hand! He turned to her. She was smiling at him.

"See, Daddy? I can make myself real if I try really hard."

Nicholas slowly reached out and brushed his fingers along her brown hair, then ran his fingers down the side of her face. She felt warm to his touch.

In that moment, he believed it all. He didn't know how it was possible, but this was his little girl, *in the flesh*!

"Oh, my God, it really is you! My darling baby!" he said as he pulled her close to him and hugged her tightly to his chest. He could smell her hair - a fresh, clean scent. He began kissing her head. "I've dreamed of this since the first day your mother told me that she was pregnant." He was crying now. "Oh, how I've wanted to hold you and love you. My darling Madeline. I love you so much!"

"Oh, Daddy, I love you, too," she said as she hugged him back as tightly as her arms would let her. "I've always been with you, Daddy. I kept throwing fits wanting to be with you, 'cause I could see how you were hurting, and it hurt me, too. But now you can hug me when you're hurting, and I can make it better!"

Nicholas looked down into her face, tears running freely down his face. "Thank you, honey. Thank you."

"You're welcome. But I have to change back now. Being real is dangerous."

"Do you have to change back, Madeline?"

She nodded. "I can only be real for a little while. It uses up a bunch of my energy. But I'll still be with you, okay?"

"Okay, my little darling child. You do what you have to."

She closed her eyes again. Gradually, the white glow surrounded her as before, then faded. When she opened her eyes again, Nicholas reached for her hand. His hand passed through her again, and again he felt that warm tingle.

"Daddy! That *tickles*!" She giggled.

"You know I've got a lot of questions, don't you, honey?"

She nodded. "I know. But you're gonna have to ask me while we're driving. You've got to talk to that man. It's important."

Nicholas smiled. "Yes, ma'am." He started the car and began driving toward the address that Snickers had given him.

"Okay, Madeline, first question. Who were you talking to when you popped back into the car?"

"It was the man in charge of letting me come here. He told me to stop telling you things I'm not sposed to. Mom told me that, too...but she winked at me when the man wasn't looking."

He smiled again. "That sounds like your mother, all right. Well, we'll do our best, won't we?"

"Yep."

"You said that you had restrictions. What are they?"

She looked disgusted. "I couldn't talk to you until you guessed who I was, but you already knew that. I'm not sposed to tell you things that are supposed to be. I'm not sposed to let anybody but you see me. I can only tell you things to help you figure out how to save Karen, but I'm not sposed to tell you why. I only have enough energy to show up for a while. I can make myself real for a little while, but it uses up a lot of energy. When I'm real, I'm just like any other little girl. I can be hurt. When I'm like this, I can't. Sometimes, I can make just part of me real." She thought for a minute. "I think that's everything...no, wait! If I die while I'm real, I can't come back again. And I'm not sposed to do anything to inter...inter..."

"Interfere?"

"Yeah, interfere. I'm not sposed to interfere with anything that happens."

"Wow. That's a lot of restrictions."

"Yeah, it's sucky."

"So you can't tell me why I need to talk to this man?"

"Uh-uh."

"Or why I needed to call Marcus?"

"Uh-uh."

"Do you know how long you can stay with me?"

She shook her head.

"So you might have to go back anytime?"

She nodded.

Nicholas took a deep breath. "Well, that sucks, too."

"It sure does."

He noticed that they were entering the industrial area. It was populated with lots of abandoned factories and warehouses. Some were in good shape, but most were beginning to look seedy and in disrepair.

"We're getting close, Madeline. I think you should fade out now, okay?"

She nodded. "But I'll still be around." She slowly faded from view.

Nicholas found the address. It was an old agricultural warehouse, with three silos close to the building - two on the left and one on the right, complete with circular stairways rising on each one. He pulled into the asphalt driveway and into the building's parking lot. Both the parking lot and the driveway had weeds springing up through cracks in the pavement, and the area was littered with soda cans, fast food bags, used condoms, and other trash. It looked as if it hadn't been used in several years. The front door was hanging from one hinge and swung open freely. Inside was what had once been a reception area, but now it looked like a junkie's crash pad. An old stained mattress was in one corner, and a rat sat on the mattress on its hind legs, looking at him. Trash was everywhere. He drew his gun.

When he found the main warehouse, he stopped just inside the door, waiting for his eyes to adjust to the darkness. The door from the office area led into the warehouse on the left side of the building. There were several large windows to his left, and he could see two silos in the gloom outside. What little light that came through the windows didn't reach very far into the vast area, but it was enough to see about ten feet. He saw a dim light coming from what looked like a small, glassed-in office area in the center of the huge building.

"Logan!" he shouted. "Ricky Logan! I'm Nicholas Turner! Are you here?"

His voice echoed in the gloom. Silence answered him. He couldn't see a thing in here, and he kept his gun ready.

"Logan! Snickers sent me to talk to you! I can help you, Logan, but you have to talk to me!"

More silence.

Nicholas was beginning to wonder if somebody had misled Snickers, when he heard a voice to his right.

"You alone, man?"

"Yes."

A piece of the darkness moved, and into the dim light stepped a figure. Ricky Logan was about five-eight, with blond hair and a scraggly beard. He had dirt on his forehead, as if he had been sleeping on the dirty floor. He was wearing a T-shirt under a pair of dirty overalls. Flecks of what looked to be white paint splattered his overalls. The man looked haunted.

"Show me some ID, man."

Nicholas held up his left hand. "I'm reaching for my license." He took out the small folded wallet that held his private investigator's license and showed it to Logan.

The man nodded.

"I heard through Snickers that you could get me some protection if I talked to you. Is that right?"

"Yes. I have a friend in the FBI. If you've got good information, he can put you someplace where you can't be found."

"That ain't enough. I want immunity, too. I've done a few things, but I don't want to go to jail for talking."

"Just how good is your information?"

"It's hot, man. I know stuff about some very high-up people. Dates, places...I got it all."

"Then my friend will make sure you've got immunity."

Logan thought for a minute. "Man, I'm really scared. Somebody's tried to kill me twice already. Looks like I ain't got a choice but to trust you." He was quiet for a few seconds, then nodded to himself as if he had made up his mind about something. "It's a deal, man." He held out his right hand to shake.

Nicholas put his gun in its holster and shook Logan's hand. "Thanks, Logan. I'll do what I can to keep you safe until my friend gets here."

"Okay, Turner, what do you want to know?"

"Snickers said that you had accepted a kidnap-to-order contract. Tell me about it."

Logan took a breath. "Yeah, man, I took the contract. I wish to God I hadn't. I'm not very proud of it." He put his hands in the pockets of his overalls and leaned against the warehouse wall. Outside the windows, the moon had come out from behind some clouds and provided enough light for Nicholas to see Logan clearly. He looked like his conscience was really bothering him. "Dude came to me, said that he heard I might be interested in earning a fat fee. I asked him for what. He said that he had some clients...that's how he said it, clients...that were interested in a particular kind of woman. They wanted a dark-haired woman, either brown or dark auburn. She had to be short and pretty, no taller than five-one, and no older than twenty-one." He paused for a minute, then went on. "They specifically wanted her to be flat-chested, as flat as I could find. Dude said that they would pay me twenty grand. I told him that I wouldn't do it for less than twenty-five. He said okay, real quick, like he was expecting it. I found out later that the woman was supposed to be for a bunch of rich guys...and they wanted her just to fuck her." He paused. "When I found that out, I started to get a bad feeling about the whole thing. I was glad my part was over."

"Did you find a girl like they wanted?"

"Oh, sure, man. That was the easy part. I just cruised the city college campus until I saw what I needed. I caught her crossing a parking lot alone, and I zapped her with a taser and put in my van. When I got her in my van, I hogtied her and put duct tape over her mouth and drove off. Then I called Dude and made delivery and got my money."

"Do you still have the phone number?"

"Nah, man. The deal was, we each had one of those throwaway cell phones...the kind you can use once and throw away. Cheap ones. Once I called him, we both got rid of them."

"What did you do with the woman?"

Logan took another deep breath. "Dude told me meet him at the rail yards. When I got there, they had this shipping container all set up for her, man. We carried her inside the container, and it had this bunk with chains attached to the wall, and the chains had handcuffs on the end, one for each hand and one for each ankle. We got her all set up, and Dude shut the container doors and locked them. Then he gave me my money."

"So they transported her by train?"

"I dunno, man. Some of those containers, they ship stuff overseas. I don't know if it went by rail or by ship. Could've been either one, but it wasn't my business then. I'd done my part, man, the rest of it was their business."

"Who was the man you contacted?"

"I didn't know then, I was just doing a job. And I'm still not sure. A couple of months later, though, he shows back up. Says that his clients had fucked out the chick I'd gotten for them. They wanted something new and they had another order for me, if I was interested. Dude said this job was worth fifty grand. I said what happened to the other one. He said that she wouldn't be fucking anybody again. I think they killed her, man, and I started to feel bad about what I'd done. I mean, fucking the chick was one thing, killing her was another. But I didn't want Dude to know that it was bothering me, because I wanted to find out as much as I could about them. I thought I could maybe give the cops some information if I had it. So I asked Dude what they wanted this time." He paused again. "Turner, he said they wanted a kid. No older than ten, pretty, and she had to have long blond hair." He ran his hand across his face. "I told Dude no way, man. I don't mess with kids, especially for something like he wanted. He asked was I sure, I said yeah. Dude left without another word. Later, when I left the bar, somebody took a shot at me. They missed, but they were *close*, man! So, I went to this friend's place to crash and hide out for a while. Everything seemed cool, until my friend decided to go pick up some food. His car exploded. When I looked out the window, I saw Dude. He was sitting in this car, only it wasn't a regular car. I think he's a..."

Logan never finished the sentence. The glass to Nicholas's left tinkled, a small hole appeared in Logan's forehead, and the back of Logan's head exploded against the wall.

Nicholas vaguely heard the shot. He drew his gun, and then heard a voice. "Duck, Daddy!"

He ducked. When he did, the glass tinkled again, and a hole appeared where his head had just been. He vaguely heard another shot. Holding close to the floor, he checked Logan's pulse, although he knew the man was dead. Nothing. He glanced at the window. He guessed that the shooter was on one of the silos, and that he had to be using a night vision scope. He duck walked quickly back the way he came until he was out of sight of the windows. Then he ran outside.

Once outside, he stopped at the corner of the building, using it for cover. He chanced a peek around the corner toward the silos, and slivers of brick showered his face, followed by the sound of the shot. He quickly ducked back behind the corner. He had seen the muzzle flash, however. He squatted, counted to three, then threw himself around the corner again, quickly firing a shot toward the spot where he had seen the flash. More brick fragments fell in the spot where his head would have been if he had been standing. He ducked back behind the corner.

Headlights swept the parking lot from left to right. A car. Marcus, thank God.

Marcus saw Nicholas, got out of the car, and ran over beside his friend.

"What's up, Nicky?"

"There's a shooter on the first silo over there. I think he's got a night vision scope on a high-powered rifle. He shot Logan, and darn near got me."

"So how do we neutralize him?"

"Go up, Daddy."

"What did you say, Nicky?"

Nicholas stammered, "Uh...I said let's try going up." Marcus had heard Madeline!

The office area jutted out from the main warehouse building for about twenty feet, and the roof was only about ten feet above them.

"Listen, Marcus, you're a better shot than I am. Why don't I boost you up to the roof, and you ease around the corner and see if you can see the shooter? He's about thirty feet up the silo. Once you're up there, I'll count to fifty, then try to draw his fire, and you take him out...alive, if you can."

"I'll try, but at this distance, I'll take what I can get."

Nicholas boosted Marcus to the roof. Once on the roof, Marcus slowly risked a peek around the corner. Slowly, so the shooter wouldn't notice movement, Marcus raised his gun and took aim.

Below, Nicholas counted. "...forty-eight...forty-nine...*fifty*!" He threw himself around the corner of the building onto the ground, firing a shot as he fell. The man with the rifle fired again, and Nicholas heard the whine of the bullet as it passed his ear. Marcus fired his gun. The shooter dropped his rifle, grabbed his right shoulder, and swayed. Then he fell over the stairway's railing, landed, and didn't move.

"Nicky!" Marcus called as he jumped off the office roof. "You okay?"

"I'm okay!" said Nicholas as he got to his feet. "Good shot, buddy - you saved my sorry butt."

"Glad to do it, my friend. Come on, let's go see if our shooter is still kicking."

They spread out and approached the man on the ground, each with their gun pointed. As they got to him, both men noticed that the shooter's head was bent at an odd angle. Marcus's bullet had struck the upper part of the shoulder and would not have killed him, but the man had broken his neck in the fall.

"Shit!" said Marcus in disgust. He looked at the shooter's face. "Do you know him, Nicky?"

Nicholas studied the man's features, but he wasn't familiar. "No."

"Where's Logan?"

"Inside the warehouse. This guy," he said, as he kicked the dead man, "shot him through the window."

Marcus had found the rifle. "You were right. A .223 with a night vision scope. You were damned lucky!"

Nicholas said, "Not lucky, just blessed." He felt a warm tingle on his cheek and smiled.

"I've got to call this in, but I don't want the city police involved if I can help it. Let me call my boss, then we'll compare notes," said Marcus. He took out his cell phone and walked away a few feet.

Nicholas walked a few feet away in the other direction, looked at Marcus, who was oblivious for the moment. He mumbled under his breath, "I thought you weren't supposed to interfere."

"Shut up, Daddy," Madeline said in a stage whisper.

"And Marcus heard you."

"Stop, Daddy!" she whispered again.

"Love you, babygirl." He felt the warm tingle on his cheek again. He smiled, and walked back toward Marcus. He was finished with his phone call.

"My boss is calling it in for us. We can't shut out the city police completely, but we can claim jurisdiction."

"Why do you want to keep the police out of it?"

"First, tell me what led you to Logan, and what he said to you."

So, Nicholas told his friend everything, beginning with saving Snickers in the bar and finishing with Marcus pulling into the parking lot. He omitted any mention of Madeline, of course. He realized that he wasn't crazy, but he wasn't sure if Marcus would believe him. Besides, she was *his* secret...and he was jealously guarding it for now.

"Great, Nicky. Now let's see if our perp has some ID."

They walked to the body, and Marcus searched it. The man had no ID.

"Of course. Professional. Guys like this carry no ID just in case something goes wrong," said Marcus. He looked at Nicholas. "The thing I wanted to tell you was that we found an old lady that lives on Richardson's street. She was looking out the window from three till three thirty the day the little girl was kidnapped. The only car she saw was a city police car making a pass through the neighborhood. She told my agent that she didn't mention it to the police because they asked her if she had seen any strange vehicles during that time. Of course she didn't."

Nicholas's eyes widened. "You think a cop kidnapped the girl?"

"Think about it, Nicky. We didn't get called in for three days. The only car passing through the neighborhood was a police car. Parker couldn't get any leads on the kidnapping. It all fits. And cops have been dirty before."

"So that's why you wanted to keep the regular police out of this."

"Yeah. If *this* guy," he nodded back toward the body, "is a cop, his prints and DNA will be on file. If the local police got involved, we run the risk of interference with the evidence. Until we know for sure that the police are involved, and if they are, how high up it goes, we need to keep things as quiet as possible."

"Agreed. But do me one favor, Marcus. When everyone arrives, please don't mention Snickers by name. I wouldn't want anything to happen to him. All anyone needs to know is that I received a tip from an informant."

"I wasn't going to mention him, Nicky. I know what he means to you. And I do want to meet him someday."

"I have a couple of people in my life that I'd like you to meet," said Nicholas. "One of them will blow your mind."

Chapter 6

THE FBI PEOPLE ARRIVED first. With their usual efficiency, the processing of the scene was well underway when the first city police arrived. The forensic team had already fingerprinted the dead men, and taken several DNA samples from both. The local police were limited to crowd control and traffic duty, both of which were unnecessary in the industrial park at three o'clock in the morning. Homicide investigators from the city police department were not angry about being shut out of the investigation of the shooting, because they had enough cases to keep them busy without adding this one to their workloads. After talking to Marcus, they left, leaving only a couple of street patrolmen to show a presence.

Both Nicholas and Marcus were interviewed, first separately, then together. Their stories were supported by the evidence, and they were able to show that the shootings were part of the ongoing investigation into the Richardson kidnapping.

Finally, at five o'clock, Marcus told Nicholas that they were both free to leave.

"What's next, Nicky?"

"I'm going to the rail yard tonight to snoop around. Want to come with?"

"You bet your buns I do. I have a feeling that we're on to something."

Nicholas's cell phone rang. Then Marcus's cell phone rang.

Nicholas answered his phone. "Nicholas Turner."

"This is Meredith. Someone has shot out my front windows."

"*What*? Are you hurt?"

"No, but can you come?" She sounded shaken.

Marcus disconnected his cell phone. "Nicky! That was the agent I left at the Richardson house. Somebody shot up the house! We've got to go!"

Nicholas nodded his understanding to Marcus, then told Meredith, "Marcus and I are on our way. Hold tight, Meredith."

"Please hurry, Nicholas. I am frightened."

"Ten minutes." He disconnected the phone.

"Let's take my car. I'll have someone bring your car later," said Marcus.

The men got into Marcus's car and sped away. Marcus turned on his siren and emergency lights.

"My agent said that he and the techs were sitting in the kitchen when they heard several shots from the front of the house," Marcus said. "They heard glass breaking, and Ms. Richardson was screaming upstairs. When my agent got out front, the shooter...or shooters...had vanished. He said that nobody was hurt, but a couple of bullets hit the bed where Ms. Richardson was sleeping. It was that close."

"She sounded really scared on the phone," Nicholas said. "That's all she needs right now. But, it proves that we're on the right track with the kidnapping."

"How so?"

"Look at it - if she's out of the picture, the pressure is off to find the kid." Nicholas had a strong sense of determination on his face. "They don't know me very well, do they?"

"That's right, isn't it? You and that damned power of attorney you make your clients sign. Karen is basically yours right now, isn't she?"

"Yes, and no daughter of mine will want for anything." Nicholas felt the warm tingle on his cheek again. "Karen has a father again, at least for now...and no real father ever stops fighting for his kid."

"What are you going to do, Nicky?"

"If you don't mind, Marcus, when we get there, I'm taking Meredith someplace safe, and I'll let you look into the shooting. I don't think they'd try shooting up her house again, but I'm not willing to take that chance. I think they're getting desperate."

"I do, too. Whoever the kidnappers are, they have no idea what you've learned, and it sounds like they're not taking any chances. And you're forgetting something, old friend."

"What's that?"

"You're probably in real danger yourself. We're here."

The front of the house was a shambles. Every window facing the street was broken, and a couple of the shutters were hanging crookedly. Some of the neighbors were outside their homes, wearing bathrobes and pajamas.

The two men got out of the car and walked to the front door.

"Notice anything?" said Marcus.

"Yeah, no police cars. You know at least one of the neighbors would have called this in."

Marcus knocked.

"Who is it?" came from behind the door.

"Moore."

The door opened. The FBI agent was putting away his gun. Nicholas shoved past him.

"Meredith!" he called. "Meredith!"

She came from the kitchen. Nicholas met her, took her into his arms, and hugged her tightly. She returned the hug.

"Are you all right?"

"I was so frightened, Nicholas."

"I'm here now."

Marcus walked past them toward the kitchen and said, "Are you two sure you don't know each other?"

They both smiled sheepishly and pulled apart. Neither of them could explain the sudden burst of feeling for each other.

"Have you found out anything about Karen?" she asked Nicholas.

"We're pretty sure we've got a good lead. We're going to check it out tonight. I'll tell you about it later. Right now, I want you to pack a bag for a couple of nights. I'm taking you someplace safe. And, before you say anything, the techs and the FBI will stay here just in case, but I don't think we're going to get any more calls from the kidnappers."

Meredith studied his face for a moment. "All right, Nicholas. I will go pack now." She went upstairs.

He went into the kitchen. The two techs, Mickey and Ronnie, were talking to Marcus. They were visibly shaken, but neither one had any desire to abandon their posts. They nodded a greeting to Nicholas as he came in.

"Nicholas, this is Agent Adams," said Marcus. They shook hands. "Tell him what you told me, Adams."

"It was definitely an automatic weapon. The bullets came too fast to be anything else. As I told Agent Moore, by the time I worked my way to the front, the shooter was gone. I called Agent Moore, then tried to secure the area as much as I could while protecting the three civilians. A city patrol car did come here, but I told them who I was and that it was an FBI matter, so they left."

"How long after the shooting did the patrol car arrive?" asked Nicholas.

"Five minutes, tops."

Nicholas nodded.

"Where's Ms. Richardson?" Marcus asked him.

"Packing for a couple of nights."

"Good. Don't tell anyone where you're taking her. I'll call you this evening and we'll look into that place we were discussing."

"Sounds good. Marcus, be careful."

"You, too. Remember what I told you."

Nicholas nodded. He walked into the foyer and stood at the foot of the stairs, waiting for Meredith. He looked around to make sure no one was close to him, then said quietly, "How am I doing, babygirl?"

"Just fine, Daddy," whispered Madeline.

He smiled. Meredith came down the stairs carrying a small sports bag. She saw him smiling, and, thinking it was for her, smiled back.

"My shining knight," she said to him.

"Maybe, but this knight's trusty steed is parked in front of a warehouse. We'll have to take your hybrid."

She took her keys out of her purse and gave them to him.

At the front door, Nicholas paused and scanned the area, then motioned for Meredith to follow him. They got into the car and drove toward Nicholas's office.

"It's the safest place for you that I can think of," he told her. "Nobody will expect me to take you there."

"Until they see my car parked at your office building."

"Not necessarily. I'm hoping to hide you in plain sight."

"What's been happening, Nicholas? Why did someone shoot at my house?"

"It's a long story, Meredith. Before I start, I need you to answer a question as honestly as you can."

"All right. Ask away."

"How do you feel about me?"

She turned to look at him. "Before I answer, I should tell you something. Last night, I asked Agent Moore about you. He told me about what happened to you all those years ago, and what you've done since. He then told me that you're a 'keeper', as he put it."

"He told me the same thing about you. I think Marcus is playing Cupid."

"You can only play Cupid if the attraction is there. In my case, it is." She sat for a minute. "I simply cannot believe that I'm discussing my attraction to you with all that is happening right now. However, to answer your question, I was never a believer in 'love at first sight.' I always thought it was simply lust or misguided hope. Until now."

She continued, "I felt like I was in love from the moment I saw you. I cannot explain it. I am not going to try. I am simply going to trust my feelings."

"I understand. I have the same feelings for you. And for Karen. I actually called her my daughter earlier, and I've never even met her." He glanced at her. "Thank you for being honest with my question. It means that I can trust you with what I'm going to tell you. Parts of this story may seem hard to believe, but it's all true. It started just before you came to the office..."

He began by telling her about waking up and seeing Madeline, and finished with what he asked her just before he and Meredith left the house a few minutes ago. While he was telling her his story, they arrived at his office building. He wrapped up the story just as he unlocked his office and they went inside.

"Let me make sure I understand you, Nicholas. You say your unborn daughter is helping you find my daughter because she says we are supposed to be together?"

"Well...yes. That's a good way to put it, I suppose."

"And because of her, you were able to keep your friend from being hurt, you found the one person that could give you a lead into Karen's whereabouts, and told you to duck when you were being shot at to save your life."

"I know it sounds crazy, Meredith."

"Crazy is not the word for it. May I please have my car keys? I will not remain in the company of a psychotic individual!"

Nicholas felt a slight breeze as he took a step toward her. "Meredith, please. Try to keep an open mind..." He stopped. A breeze? From where? It seemed to be getting stronger...

"An open mind?" Meredith shouted. The breeze began turning into a wind. A couple of papers blew off of the desk. The leaves of the ficus tree began to agitate. "Your open mind apparently allowed in something crazy!"

"Meredith, I think you'd better stop," Nicholas said.

"Stop?! Stop what? Your faulty air conditioning? Or stop noticing that you're crazy?"

"MY DADDY IS NOT CRAZY!" shouted Madeline, seemingly from everywhere. "I'LL SHOW YOU CRAZY, YOU MEAN OLD THING!"

"Madeline, NO!" shouted Nicholas. He was having a hard time being heard over the roar of the wind inside the office. Papers were blowing everywhere. The ficus tree fell over. "Stop this tantrum now, little girl!"

The wind stopped abruptly. Papers fell to the floor.

Meredith had a look of incredulity on her face. "What in the name of heaven was that?"

"Are you all right?" he asked Meredith. She looked at him with wide eyes and nodded. "Good. Madeline! Show yourself, and I mean *right now*!"

Madeline faded into view. She was standing with her arms crossed between Nicholas and Meredith, looking up at Meredith with an angry look.

"Daddy, I'm mad at her," Madeline said. "You're not crazy, she is."

He reached for her and his hand passed through her again. He barely registered the warm tingle.

"Apologize to Meredith."

"No."

"Madeline Louise, you will apologize right now."

"But, Daddy..."

"Now."

She stomped her foot and turned to Meredith. "I'm sorry," she said with her arms crossed, looking down at the floor.

"It is all right. I am quite sorry, too," said Meredith, wide-eyed. "Nicholas, I...I do not feel well..." She slumped to the floor.

"Daddy, why does everybody faint when I come around?"

Nicholas started laughing as he picked Meredith up. He carried her back to his living area and put her gently on his sofa. Madeline followed. He went to the bathroom and soaked a washcloth with cold water. He returned to Meredith and put it on her forehead. He was still chuckling.

"What's so funny, Daddy?"

"I was just laughing at the look on your face when you faded in just now."

"It's not funny," said Madeline. She was starting to smile herself. Then she started giggling. "I guess I did look funny, didn't I? But I was so mad at Meredith, I couldn't help it!"

They were both laughing now. Nicholas did an imitation of Madeline's angry look, which made Madeline giggle even harder. Then Madeline overacted Meredith's reaction, and they both laughed even harder.

"I hope you two are enjoying yourselves," said Meredith. "It has been a while since I was the object of such ridicule."

Nicholas and Madeline both looked surprised at being caught by Meredith. They both burst out laughing again. Meredith sat up, folded the washcloth, then started chuckling. Soon, all three were laughing.

A few minutes later they had semi-composed themselves.

Nicholas asked Meredith, "Well, do you still think I'm crazy?"

"Perhaps, but not because of your daughter. I believe what I see. Madeline," said Meredith. "Will you come closer to me, please?"

Madeline came to the sofa and stood in front of Meredith. Nicholas watched from the dining table. This was their time, and he wouldn't intrude. Meredith reached for the child's hand. She, too, felt a warm tingle when her hand passed through Madeline's. She tried again with the same result. She looked into Madeline's eyes.

"How is Karen, Madeline?"

"She's okay. She hasn't been hurt, if that's what you mean. She's scared, but she knows Daddy...I mean she's not too worried."

Meredith looked at Nicholas. He nodded. He had caught it, too.

"How does she know that your daddy is looking for her?"

Madeline looked uncomfortable. "I dunno."

"Madeline, did you tell her about your daddy? Can you talk to her?"

Madeline looked at Nicholas. "Dad-dee," she said pleadingly.

"Answer the question, babygirl."

60

She looked at the floor and nodded. "I told her."

"Can you talk to her just anytime?"

Madeline nodded.

"Do you have to leave here to talk to Karen?"

She nodded again.

"Will you tell her something from me?"

"I guess so."

"Please tell her that I love her very much, and that we're coming to get her as soon as we can. Can you remember that?"

"Sure! Do you want me to go now?"

"In a minute, Madeline. I have another favor to ask of you."

"Okay, Meredith. What?"

Meredith looked at Nicholas. He gestured to her as if to say that it was between the two of them. She turned back to Madeline.

"Your father told me that you can make yourself 'real', as you put it. Can you do that for me now?"

Madeline nodded. "But I can't stay that way long. It uses up a lot of energy."

"I know it does. I won't keep you that way long."

Madeline closed her eyes and concentrated. The white glow began surrounding her again as it did when she changed for Nicholas earlier. It grew very bright, and seemed to come from both inside and outside of the child. As it paled, Madeline opened her eyes.

Meredith reached for Madeline's hands and looked into her eyes. "Thank you. For comforting Karen, for bringing your father and I together, for helping us...thank you."

Madeline smiled. "You're welcome, Meredith," she said. She leaned close to Meredith and stage whispered, "You make Daddy very happy. He'll tell you if you ask him."

Meredith laughed. "I will ask him, darling. And as for you, to show you that I forgive you for your tantrum, I have something for you." Meredith quickly pulled the child into her arms and began tickling her. Madeline laughed and squirmed. Meredith laughed and kept tickling her. After a moment, she stopped tickling Madeline, hugged her tight, then kissed her cheek.

"You are a darling, Madeline. I am sorry I doubted you or your father."

"It's okay, Meredith. I better change back now."

"All right."

"Wait a minute," said Nicholas. "I don't want to waste a 'real' minute. C'mere, you!"

Madeline ran to her father's arms and hugged him tight. He kissed one cheek, then the other.

"Better change back, babygirl," he told her.

" 'kay." She closed her eyes again. The glow appeared and disappeared. She opened her eyes. "I'll go see Karen now. I guess you two want to be alone, don't you?"

"Scram, kid," said Nicholas.

Madeline smiled and faded out.

Nicholas went to the sofa and sat down beside Meredith.

"You okay?" he asked.

"As well as can be expected considering the circumstances. It is very overwhelming, isn't it?"

"You're not kidding. You're taking it very well considering it's only been about an hour for you. I've only known about her for about twelve hours, and I'm still overwhelmed."

"You realize the implications of her presence, don't you, Nicholas? She's the answer to everyone's question as to whether there is life after death, whether there is a higher power...name your theological question, Madeline is the answer."

Nicholas nodded. "You're right. But she raises many more questions than she answers, Meredith. You saw what she did when she was angry at you. It makes me wonder how powerful she really is...and if she's that powerful, if I can I keep her power reigned in when I'm only able to touch her when she makes herself 'real'. Nobody gave me an instruction manual when she showed up."

"What is she, Nicholas? I mean, I know *who* she is, but *what* is she?"

"She's not a ghost. I asked her that, and she said she wasn't. I guess that's true. How can you be ghost if you've never been born?" He thought for a minute. "I think it's her soul. I think her soul was maybe...assigned...to her when she was conceived. Then, when for whatever reason, the fetus miscarried, she chose to remain with first her mother, and now me. And maybe I'm oversimplifying things, but I think I'm right about it."

"Did you have any idea that she had been talking to Karen?"

He shook his head. "No. There's a lot going on with Madeline that I wonder about. She came to me with 'restrictions', but she's broken several of them already, and nothing has happened to her. She's still here, and apparently hasn't been punished for anything." He suddenly remembered the way she had appeared in the car. It had seemed as if she was arguing with someone, and her sentence ended with, "you can't make me." He related this to Meredith.

"What do you think it means, Nicholas?"

He snickered. "If she's anything like me, I think it means she's gone rogue. She's doing what she damn well pleases, and doesn't care who likes it. Jane had a streak of that, too, but it wasn't as strong as it is with me." He leaned back against the couch and rubbed his eyes. "Damn, I'm tired. I've been on the go for almost twenty-four hours."

Meredith leaned over and put her head on his chest. "Do you think we will get Karen back soon?"

He said tiredly, "I think so. Things are coming to a head pretty quickly. The kidnappers have made several mistakes, and they're getting desperate. Marcus and I are checking out the rail yard tonight. Another plus is our little secret weapon. You know, I'm wondering about her ability to change into a 'real' girl..."

She asked quietly, "Do you think she's right about you and I?"

Nicholas didn't answer. He was fast asleep.

Chapter 7

NICHOLAS WAS DREAMING.

He was at the picnic again, and still had his head in Jane's lap.

"Nicholas," said Jane.

"Um-hmm," he replied.

"You're right about Madeline. She's decided to remain with you."

"That's good, Janey. I need her."

"And she needs you. But I'm worried about her. We all have free will, which means the choice to remain is hers."

"So what's the problem? Why are you worried?"

"Her situation is unique, Nicholas. If she had had a normal life and passed on naturally, once here, she would not have been allowed to come to you, except as I have - in dreams. If her soul had not been assigned to her fetus, the situation would not have arisen.

"Most souls in her situation choose to be reassigned to another fetus. She chose to remain as who she would have been had she been born. Her soul has continued to age as if she were an actual child, and will continue to do so until she chooses to be reassigned. What worries me is that she has all the power of those that are called angels in your world, and she has no idea what power she has - and she has free will. She can't be called back unless she chooses to come back, nor can her power be restricted. Only she has the choice to come back here."

"Unless her 'real' self dies."

Nicholas let that sink in for a moment. He sat up and looked at Jane.

"Are you asking me to get her killed?"

"It's an option to be considered."

"No, it isn't." He stood up and said firmly, "For the first time in her life *and* mine, Madeline and I have a chance to spend time as father and daughter. I will *never* make that choice for her.

"It sounds to me like somebody up here is regretting giving me this 'gift'. Well, boo-hoo, *too bad*! She's my gift, and I won't give her up. I was cheated out of a happy life when I lost you and Madeline. Now I've got another chance with Meredith and Karen, and I've got my own daughter, too. I may be selfish, but I will *not* give any of it up...and I can't believe you, of all people, would ask me to, Jane."

"She was only sent to help you with Meredith and Karen. She doesn't belong there, Nicholas."

"So what?"

Jane smiled. "I was told to try to reason with you, Nicky. I did. Now, for myself, I approve of Meredith, and I'm very happy for you. I knew you wouldn't give her up, and I'm glad for that. Your stubborn streak is one of the reasons I fell in love with you. Love our daughter, husband of mine. It looks like you're going to have her for a while. And good luck."

Nicholas woke up. He was lying on the couch with a blanket over him. He heard laughter from the office. He kicked back the blanket, got up, and went to see what was so funny.

Meredith and Madeline were in the office, giggling. When he appeared in the doorway, Meredith said, "Well. Look who's back among the living!"

Madeline giggled at the remark.

Nicholas said, "That's truer than you think. What time is it?"

"Three o'clock," said Meredith.

"What are you two up to out here?"

Meredith looked at Madeline. "Should we show him?"

Madeline nodded. "Watch, Daddy."

He leaned against the doorframe and watched his daughter. She glowed brightly, making herself 'real'. There were a number of full soda cans on the desk. Madeline put her hand on one, then closed her eyes and changed back. She took her hand off of the soda.

"Have a drink, Daddy," she said.

Giving her a suspicious look, he reached for the soda can she had touched.

His hand passed through the can. Twice. Both Meredith and Madeline giggled.

"Meredith said that I should do that to a chair and tell you to sit down. I told her that would be mean." Then she giggled again. "But it would have been funny, Daddy."

Nicholas barely heard her. Madeline had changed something real into something transparent! *She had moved a real object into the spirit world that she existed in!* If she could do that with a soda can...the implications were staggering! He pulled the client chair around so that he could sit down. *Holy crap!* he thought. *Can she only do it with small things? Could she do it with a chair, or a car, or...*

"Nicholas? Are you all right?" asked Meredith.

"You're not mad at me, are you, Daddy?" asked Madeline.

He shook his head. "Madeline, come here." She walked over and stood in front of him, looking puzzled.

"Did I do something wrong, Daddy?" she asked.

"No, baby, not at all," he replied. "I have something serious to ask you." He gestured to the soda can. "Can you do that with a person?"

Meredith looked surprised. Madeline looked scared.

"Daddy, I'm not sposed to. That's a restriction."

"So what, Madeline? You've got free will, and you've already used it by choosing to stay with me, haven't you?"

She nodded.

"And no one can make you go back if you don't want to, can they?"

She shook her head.

"So who cares if it's a restriction? They can't make you come back if you don't want to, and they can't take your powers away. Am I right?"

"Yes. But, Daddy..."

"Wait a minute, honey. You said that making yourself 'real' uses up a lot of power, but I haven't seen any evidence of it. Is that something you were told before you came here?"

She nodded.

"Guess what, Madeline...I think they lied to you."

Meredith gasped. "Nicholas! What are you saying?"

"I just had a chat with Jane..."

"You talked to Mom again?"

Nicholas nodded, then continued, "She said that the powers that be wanted me to..." He paused. "To talk Madeline into coming back, because she has free will and has chosen to stay here with me, and *they can't make her do anything that she doesn't want to do.* Of course, I refused, because it's time for me to be selfish, both for myself and for Madeline.

"But they're worried. Madeline apparently has enormous powers because of her situation. Jane compared it to the power of what we call 'angels'. Since she had chosen to come back, she was told that she had restrictions on what she could do while she was here, counting on the fact that she is basically a little girl, trusting what they told her.

"Maybe they didn't lie to her, but they did mislead her."

"Nicholas," said Meredith. "Why would they mislead her?"

"I don't know for sure, but my guess would be to keep the human race from knowing that there is life after death. Maybe to keep the whole mystery of life from becoming common knowledge."

Turning to Madeline, who had been listening with growing frustration, he said, "And that's what we'll do, Maddy. We'll keep you mostly a secret. We'll use your powers when we need to, but we won't explain them, and we'll lie if we have to. Your mother told me that you made the choice to remain as you were assigned, and that you chose to grow as if you had been born. That makes you a little girl of ten, with all of the impulses and growing pains that go with being that age. I think that, inside, you still retain a maturity that you had when you were created, so I think that, deep down, you're going to understand what I'm about to say. You are going to have to trust me to make decisions for you, and sometimes those decisions may go against what you want to do. You have to stay here and allow yourself to be directed as if you were a real little girl. Can you do that? Can you trust me, and Meredith, to make decisions for you?"

Madeline thought for a minute, and said, "You're right, Daddy. And I can trust you guys...I knew that before I came here. You've got a deal."

"One question. The soda can - can you change it back?"

"Of course, Daddy. That's easy."

Nicholas said, "Okay, babygirl. Here's what I want you to do." He took a deep breath. "Change me over."

"Nicholas, no!" said Meredith. "What you are considering is foolhardy and could be dangerous. These are things we are not supposed to know about! You do not know what it will do to you!"

To Meredith he said, "I think I do know what it will do to me. I'm the guinea pig." To Madeline he said, "One more question. Will I be able to pass through walls and go where I want?"

"You'll be a soul-essence, just like me. You'll be able to make yourself invisible and go anywhere you want just by thinking about it. You just won't have all of my powers."

"Do it, babygirl."

Madeline closed her eyes and made herself 'real'. She opened them and looked at Nicholas. "Daddy, are sure you're ready for this?" He nodded. "Okay, Daddy, give me your hands and close your eyes." He did.

As Meredith watched, Madeline closed her eyes. The white glow enclosed both of them and seemed to shine brighter than it ever had before. To Meredith, the glow lasted longer than it did normally. It gradually faded.

To Nicholas, it was as if he were being bathed in a friendly warmth that gave him goosebumps at the same time. He felt peaceful, and he could feel Madeline's love flowing over him like a warm wave on a beach. When the glow faded, he still felt all of it. He could also feel Meredith's worry, and he could feel her love for Karen, Madeline, and himself. It was an incredible and indescribable feeling. Madeline let go of his hands.

"Daddy, you can open your eyes now. I'm right here if you need me."

Nicholas opened his eyes to a world of light. He drew in a quick breath. Everything around him shone with light in a plethora of bright colors. The desk, the computer, the filing cabinets all shone bright pale blue. Meredith was surrounded by a white glow that gradually changed to a thick pale yellow band, then a dark blue as it grew closer to her body. Orbs of light of all the colors imaginable passed in and out of the office, going through walls as if they weren't there. Occasionally, a figure recognizable as human would pass through going up or down. He noticed that the ones moving upward were surrounded by bright colors, and the ones moving downward were shining in extremely dark colors. It was more beautiful than he could ever hope to describe. Then he looked at Madeline.

She was still Madeline, but she was surrounded by a pale white glow. From the point where her shoulders met the base of her neck, bright white light cascaded to the left and the right all the way to the floor. The cascading lights were not wings, but looked remarkably like them. The blue in her eyes glowed with an intensity that normally would have hurt his eyes to see.

"Oh, Madeline, you are so beautiful," said Nicholas. "Everything is so incredibly beautiful! Is this how you see things all the time?"

She nodded. "Except when I'm 'real', Daddy."

"The colors are so vibrant. What do they all mean?"

"Look at Meredith, Daddy, and I'll tell you. The outside whiteness is her goodness. See how wide it is? That means she's a good person. The wide yellow band is her love for all of us - Karen, you, and me. The dark blue closest to her body is her worry. She's worried for Karen and for you." She gestured to the office. "Everything has an aura around it, even things like a desk or a soda can. Everything in here has a pale blue light to it, because you use them to do good things.

"The orbs you see passing through are messengers. They're not quite what you call 'angels', but they're close. They pass messages from those in charge to people that are doing their work here on earth. Random acts of kindness often result from a brush with one of them. The brighter the color, the more goodness is contained in the message. Try not to interfere with a dark-colored orb, though. They obviously serve a darker power. They can cause random acts of violence and horror if you accidentally touch one."

"Your lips aren't moving."

"We're communicating telepathically."

"You sound different...more mature."

"That's because I'm more than just Madeline here. I'm the sum of you, Mom, and myself."

Nicholas indicated the lights cascading from her shoulders. "What are those, Madeline?"

"Those represent my energy and life force. Before I was conceived, I was what you would refer to as an 'angel'. It had been so long since I had been assigned to a person, I chose to be assigned to you and Mom because of a number of things, and the potential the two of you carried. You weren't the only one treated unfairly when my host body miscarried and my chosen mother died.

"The potential that you and Mom carried is present again, Daddy, with you and Meredith. Look at your shoulders."

Nicholas looked first right, then left. He, too, had light cascading from shoulders, although they weren't as bright or as full as Madeline's.

"How can I have these, babygirl? I'm no angel."

"If you continue on the path you're following, the potential is there for you to become one. Those people who do extraordinary good usually become one."

"This is fantastic! Meredith, you should see this!"

"She can't see or hear us, Daddy. We're on a plane of existence that human eyes can't register. I took you higher than you intended for me to take you, so that you could have some insight into who and what your daughter really is, to give you hope for the future, and to show you what your good works are destined to give you. When we go back to a slightly lower plane, she'll be able to see and hear us, and no time will have passed."

A human-like figure passed through the office, moving diagonally upwards, bathed in a pale yellow light.

"What are the human figures passing through here, Madeline?"

"What do you think they are?"

"I think they're...people that have just died, and are on their way to where you came from."

"Very good, but not all are going to the good. Remember that the darker colored orbs serve another power? It's the same way with those that have died. If they're surrounded by a dark color, they're going somewhere else."

Nicholas looked around in wonder. He didn't want to go back yet...hell, he never wanted to go back. He thought of a couple of more questions for his daughter.

"Two questions for you, babygirl: First, how do you move from one place to another?"

She smiled at him. "I know where you're going with this, but I'll answer your questions anyway. I think of where I want to be, or who I want to see. To think it is to be there."

"Can you transport someone that you change over?"

"Yes."

"You know what I'm going to ask you to do, don't you?"

"Yes. I'm surprised it took you this long, Daddy."

"I hate to leave this, but I guess it's time for us to change back."

She nodded. "Close your eyes and give me your hands."

The change back was like being pulled from a warm bed and thrown into a cold shower. Nicholas felt the warmth that had surrounded him abruptly leave him, and when he was aware of his body again, it seemed as if it were a cage. When he opened his eyes, everything was back to normal. Madeline still had his hands in hers. He pulled her close to him and held her tightly.

"Thank you, darling daughter," he whispered in her ear. "That was a wonderful gift."

"You're welcome, Daddy. I love you."

"I love you, too, babygirl."

Meredith was watching them intently. "I am waiting for someone to explain what just happened, please."

"Meredith, it was fantastic," said Nicholas. "The world is full of light and colors, with things happening all around us that defy description. I can't think of words that are sufficient to explain it. One thing is true, though...we do have an angel among us.

"Madeline, I want you to change back to your 'unreal' self right now."

"Why?"

"I'll explain after you do it, honey. 'Kay?"

" 'Kay." She closed her eyes and changed, and opened them again.

"One of the things we know is that you can be hurt or even killed when you change yourself into a 'real' girl. Whatever the higher beings are, be they God or Karma or whoever, they want you back where you came from. They instructed your mother to encourage me to try to get you killed, so that you will actually become a spirit instead of a soul-essence. I point-blank refused. You made the choice to stay, and you'll make the choice to leave...but only when you're ready to go.

"So. That's apparently the only time you're vulnerable. We'll try our best to limit your vulnerability. You only change when you can be protected. Period. Understood?"

"Yes, Daddy."

"Now, on the other hand, here's what I need you to do right now: Go to Karen, change her like you did me, and bring her here. But do it only if you can do it without being seen by anyone except her. Do you understand?"

"Yes, Daddy."

"Madeline, be careful."

"I will, Daddy. Be back in a minute!" She grinned gleefully and faded out.

Meredith had a stunned look on her face. "My God, Nicholas! Is it going to be that easy?"

He went to her and held her. "I hope so, Meredith. She travels by thought, so it shouldn't take her long to bring Karen here. I got the idea as soon as I saw you two playing with the soda cans. If Madeline can rescue Karen, Karen will be able to ID her kidnappers. Marcus and I will mop up after that."

"What happens then, Nicholas?"

"After the kidnappers are arrested, then we go to trial. You and especially Karen will have to testify in court as to the kidnapping itself."

"How will we explain the rescue? We will not be able to say that your 'angel' daughter transported her away from them."

He thought for a minute. "I'll work out some kind of story that both Karen and I will be able to remember, and we'll stick to that. Right now, I'm more worried about getting Karen back safely. Everything else will fall into place."

They sat down in the office chairs and waited. Meredith got a tissue from the box and wiped her eyes. Occasionally, Nicholas reached over and squeezed her hand. Nicholas stood up and paced around the office a couple of times, then sat down again. He and Meredith tried to talk, but both were so preoccupied that a conversation was impossible. Meredith had twisted her tissue into an unrecognizable mess, so she dropped it into the wastebasket. Nicholas again paced around the office.

After fifteen minutes had gone by, Meredith asked, "Should it take this long?"

"I don't know, but I wouldn't think so. She must have run into trouble."

"Oh, God, Nicholas, I cannot take much more! Now I am worried about *both* girls!"

"So am I. Let me try something," he said. "Madeline!" he called. "Can you hear me, babygirl?" He waited a minute. No answer. "Madeline! Answer me, honey!"

Madeline faded in. "Daddy, I couldn't get to her! They're moving her! That's what took so long!"

"Moving her? Where?"

"They took her to the rail yard, Daddy, and I can't get to her without somebody seeing me. They're guarding her like they're about to do something with her."

She looked sidelong at Meredith. "She was crying, Daddy, and he slapped her." Meredith sat down hard in her chair. "I got mad and wanted to do something, but I remembered what you told me."

"You did fine, honey. But who slapped her?"

"That cop you met at Meredith's. Parker. He's in charge, and he's got four other cops with him. One of them is that cop that gave you the ticket. Martin."

Chapter 8

MEREDITH HAD A TEAR running slowly down her cheek. Nicholas saw it, and his heart was heavy. It also strengthened his resolve.

"Time to go get her. I'm through messing around with this," he said.

"I am coming with you," said Meredith.

"No, you're not, Meredith. It's way too dangerous. I need you here so that I can know you're safe."

"She is my daughter, Nicholas."

"And she's going to be mine. Let me please do my job without having to worry about you."

She looked into his eyes and nodded. "All right. Bring her to me."

He turned to Madeline. "You, however, are coming with me. Your orders are to stay invisible and watch Karen. The first chance you have to transport her safely, you take it, and don't worry about me. Do you understand?"

"Yes, Daddy."

Nicholas picked up the phone on the desk and dialed Marcus's cell phone.

"Marcus Moore."

"It's Nicky. We have to move fast. I know where Karen Richardson is, and I know who two of the kidnappers are."

"Talk to me. I'm walking to the car now."

"Karen is at the rail yards. The leader of the kidnappers is Detective George Parker. He has a group of four other cops with him. One of them is Patrolman Jason Martin. I think they're getting ready to ship her out."

"Where are you, Nicky?"

"My office."

"I'll be there in five minutes, Nicky."

"I'll be waiting."

He hung up. "You heard what I told him, right?" he asked Meredith.

She nodded.

"If for any reason I don't make it back, you get in touch with the Chief of Police and tell him those two names and what they did. Madeline will get her chance to bring Karen here, and when she does, you take care of both girls. I'm sure Marcus is calling in what I've told him to the FBI." He drew his gun, checked the ammunition, and put more ammunition into his pants pocket. He put the gun in its holster and looked at Madeline.

"When you changed me over, we talked telepathically," he said to her. *Can you read my mind?* he thought hard.

She nodded and said, "Yes, Daddy, I can read your mind."

"Good. Then stay alert - it may be the only way I can communicate a plan to you. Let's go outside and wait for Marcus." He leaned over and kissed Meredith. "I love you, lady."

"I love you, too, Nicholas Turner."

"Spare key for the office door is in the middle drawer of the desk. Don't leave until Madeline is back with Karen. When you go, head straight to the FBI office and wait for word from us. Maddy-cat, go invisible, and let's go."

Madeline faded out as Nicholas went out the door and locked it behind him.

He arrived outside just as Marcus pulled into the parking lot.

"Let's go, Marcus. I don't think we don't have a lot of time."

Marcus sped away toward the rail yards. "How did get your information? Did Snickers come through with something?"

"I'll explain it all to you later, Marcus. Right now, let's just say that I got some inside information. Have you called it in to the Bureau?"

"The place will be crawling with agents in about forty-five minutes."

They're putting her in a container now, Daddy, Nicholas heard inside his head.

"We don't have forty-five minutes."

Marcus looked at his friend. "And how the fuck do you know that?"

"Marcus, I just...Look, we're two minutes away. I don't have enough time to tell you, but I'll give you a Show and Tell when this is over. I promise. Just trust me right now, okay?"

"I always have, Nicky."

"And if you should see anything...unusual...while this is going down, try hard to ignore it. It's all part of the explanation."

Marcus looked at his friend with an odd look on his face and continued driving.

Have they sealed the container, Madeline? Nicholas thought.

No. Tell Marcus to keep driving, Daddy. I'll guide you to where they are.

Gotcha, babygirl.

They were at the entrance gate to the rail yards. A chain-link fence with a security gate with a small kiosk surrounded the yards. There were rail cars parked on sidings, waiting to be assigned to trains that would carry them to their destinations. Shipping containers were stacked in rows three and four high all over the yards, and many were centered around the huge crane that lifted the containers from eighteen wheel trucks that brought them in, loaded and ready to be placed on a rail car for transport. Empties that would be lifted and placed back on the trucks were also scattered around the crane. There were many four-foot wide alleyways between the container stacks, to allow forklifts and other equipment access between the containers. Two police cruisers and an unmarked police car were parked just inside the gate.

"There's the police cars, Nicky."

"I see them. Listen, don't stop. I'll guide you to where you need to go."

"What, do you have a crooked cop GPS inside you or something?"

"Something like that," Nicholas said with a small smile.

Turn right at the first row of containers.

"Turn right at the first row of containers."

Marcus squealed the car into a right turn.

Turn left just after the crane.

"Turn left just past the crane."

The car swerved into a left turn.

Twelve rows up, turn right again. They're five rows up after you turn.

"Twelve rows up, turn right. They'll be five rows up after the turn."

There are only three cops at the container. I don't know where Parker and Martin are, Daddy. I'm staying close to Karen.

Be careful, babygirl, Nicholas thought.

"Marcus, there are three cops at the container with the little girl. Parker and Martin are not within sight. When we get to them, we'll take the three cops.

Then I'll try to find Parker. Don't worry about Karen. I already have a plan in place to get her to safety."

Marcus negotiated the last turn, going as fast as he could and still keep control of the car. The three cops were standing in front of an open container as the car bore down on them, mouths open in surprised "O"s. Marcus slammed on the brakes, and both he and Nicholas leaped out of the car, guns drawn, using the doors for cover.

"FBI! FREEZE!" shouted Marcus. "HANDS UP! NOW!"

Caught flatfooted, two of the cops raised their hands above their heads. The third cop reached for his gun. Marcus shot him just above the left eye, and the cop dropped like a stone.

"ON THE GROUND, ASSHOLES! NOW!"

The other two cops very carefully laid facedown on the ground. Nicholas and Marcus slowly made their way to them, took their weapons, and handcuffed them with their own cuffs.

"Nicky, that shot will have alerted the other two, so be careful. It's like a maze in here."

Nicholas nodded, then went just inside the container door. Karen Richardson was lying on a bunk bolted to the side of the container. Her wrists were chained above her head and her ankles were chained to the floor. She had duct tape over her mouth, and she had been crying.

"Karen?" said Nicholas.

The little girl nodded.

"I'm Nicholas."

Her eyes widened.

"Madeline is going to take you to Meredith. Will you trust her?"

She nodded again.

"Good girl. When I get back, I want a big hug. Okay?"

She nodded again.

"Madeline!" called Nicholas.

Madeline faded in, standing beside Karen.

"Hi, Daddy!"

"Hi, babygirl," he said. "It's time to get her out of here."

"Who's this?" said Marcus from behind him.

"Shit, Marcus, you startled me!"

"Don't swear, Daddy."

"Daddy?" said Marcus.

Nicholas shook his head, resigned. "This isn't how I wanted to show you, Marcus, but...remember the little girl I told you that I saw in my office? Marcus, meet your goddaughter. This is Madeline."

Marcus looked from Nicholas to Madeline, puzzled. "Madeline? You have a daughter you haven't told me about, buddy?" He gave Madeline a closer look. Realization began to show on his face. "My God, Nicky, she looks a lot like Jane...but how...what..."

"You're about to see something else, too. Madeline, take Karen to Meredith now. I'm going hunting. Marcus, we'll answer all of your questions later." Nicholas left the container.

Behind him, he heard Marcus say, "Where is that glow coming from?" He smiled.

Walking over to the two handcuffed cops, Nicholas said, "I don't suppose you fine gentlemen would want to tell me where to find Parker and Martin, would you?"

"Fuck you, Turner," said one of them.

"You can suck my dick, asshole," said the other.

Nicholas nodded. "That's cool. But let me point out a couple of things to you. You're handcuffed, and you're going to jail for kidnapping at the very least. That's *Federal* prison, gentlemen. Your friend there," he said as he indicated the dead cop, "isn't going anywhere, except maybe to Hell. If I were you two, I sure wouldn't want to go to prison alone. If you make it to prison, of course. See, you're both stuck here right out in the open." He waved his arm around. "Somewhere out here are two guys that know you can testify against them, and they're both armed...*and they know we have you.* We have a few minutes before the FBI takes you away." He paused. "Your friend may not be the only one going to Hell." He started to walk away. "Good luck, gentlemen."

"Wait a minute, Turner," said the first cop.

"Shut UP, you idiot!" said the second.

"You want to stay out here and let that fuckin' Parker pick you off? Not me," said the first. "Turner, move me into some cover, and I'll tell you where they went."

"Nope. You tell me first, then you get moved."

"They were going to call the guy that hired us, then they were going to the rail office to arrange shipment of the container."

"Who hired you?"

"I don't know. Parker never told us. I think he was afraid we'd try to take over or something. Now, move us, dammit!"

Nicholas pulled the first cop to his feet, then the second. As he walked them toward the open container, a shot sounded and the second cop staggered, but kept to his feet. They all began running. Another shot sounded, but it hit the ground behind them. They reached the safety of the container and the cop that had been shot fell to the floor. He had been shot in the thigh, and it was bleeding.

Marcus had drawn his gun. Nicholas tore a strip of cloth from the first cop's pants and wrapped it around the second cop's wound.

"Where did the shots come from?" asked Marcus.

"Don't know. I was too busy moving these guys to notice."

"Parker or Martin? Or both?"

"Probably Martin. Parker most likely is making himself scarce."

"One of us needs to go after Martin, Nicky."

"I know. It'll have to be me. You're the arresting officer of these two."

"You know you have some serious explaining to do about what I saw happen in here, don't you?"

"Oh, yeah."

"So get back in one piece, then. Go. I'll try to give you some cover if it's needed."

Nicholas took a breath and ducked out of the container.

Madeline and Karen faded in directly in front of Meredith. Karen still had the duct tape on her mouth, but her eyes were wide with wonder. Meredith shrieked with delight and ran to hug the girls, but passed right through them.

"Hang on, Meredith," said Madeline. She closed her eyes and changed Karen and herself 'real' again.

Meredith swept both girls into her arms. She began kissing them alternately, talking to them all the while.

"Karen" *smack* "Madeline" *smack* "I was so" *smack* "worried!" *smack* "You are both" *smack* "safe now!" *smack* "Are either of you" *smack* "hurt?" *smack*

Madeline giggled. "Meredith, you're tickling us!" She giggled again. "We might want to get the tape off of Karen's mouth pretty soon. She's got a lot to tell you."

Meredith looked closely at Karen. "Oh, baby, I am so sorry!" Karen rolled her eyes. "Here, let's try to get that off." She started gradually peeling the tape off of Karen's mouth. Finally, she pulled quickly.

"Owww, Mo-om! That hurt!" said Karen.

"Oh, I am so sorry, sweetheart," Meredith replied.

"Mom! You should see what Madeline showed me!" said Karen. "It's sooo beautiful, Mom, and sooo peaceful!"

Meredith looked at Karen, mystified.

Madeline nudged Karen. "She doesn't want to hear about that yet, ding-dong! She wants to know what happened with those bad men."

"Oh. Okay. Sorry, Mom," said Karen. "I was walking home from Amanda's, and a police car pulled up beside me. It stopped, and two policemen got out. They asked me where I was going, and I said, 'home', and then one of them grabbed me and threw me in the trunk. We drove and drove. When we stopped, we were at this house. They took me in and locked me in a room in the basement. Then this other man came. He said he was a policeman, but he didn't have on policeman's clothes. He was wearing a suit. He called me his retirement fund, whatever that is. One of the other policemen called him Parker," Meredith gasped at this, "And Parker said I'd be getting out of that room real soon. Then Madeline started coming in and talking to me. She said it would be okay. She said that her daddy was looking for me and that you were real worried and you and her daddy had fallen in love and that he would save me and make sure that those bad policemen were punished. Then today those policemen took me to a place with lots of railroad cars and Madeline's daddy stopped the policemen that were there and I met this nice FBI man. Then Madeline turned me into a ghost and brought me here." She paused. "Where are we?"

"We're in Daddy's office. And I didn't turn you into a *ghost*," said Madeline.

"Oh."

"It was a soul-essence."

"What's that?"

"Girls, save the arguments for later, okay?" Meredith hugged Karen tightly again. Then she turned to Madeline and hugged her tightly. "Thank you," she whispered into Madeline's ear.

Madeline hugged her back and whispered into Meredith's ear. "You're welcome, Meredith." Then she kissed Meredith's cheek. "I love you."

"I love you, too, little angel," Meredith replied. "Where is your father? Is he coming?"

"He only stopped three of the bad cops. Parker and Martin were still loose when I left with Karen."

Meredith's heart sank at the news. It must have shown on her face, because Karen, trying to make her mother not worry, said, "Mom, Madeline said that you and Daddy were going to get married and that he'd be my daddy, too, and she'd be my sister. And she said we'd all be happy together."

"She's right, honey," said Meredith. "I do not know how I know that I want to spend the rest of my life with Nicholas, but I do. And I know that he will love us both. And Madeline, too."

Madeline was fidgeting. "Meredith, you're not going to like this."

"Like what, honey?"

"I'm going back. Daddy's going to need help again."

Meredith opened her mouth to tell Madeline that she was to do no such thing, but she closed it again. She was getting an idea. Nicholas might be angry, but she had her own score to settle with Parker. The man had been in her *house*, putting on a façade of searching for her daughter when he had been the reason for her worry all along. How dare he put her family in danger? How dare he try to sell her daughter into sexual slavery, perhaps even worse? Oh, she had a score to settle, all right!

"Madeline, we are *all* going. Change us."

When Nicholas ducked out of the container, he broke left. Unless Martin was someplace high up, he couldn't have a clear shot as long as Nicholas was between the rows of containers. If Martin didn't have a rifle, and was using his handgun, his range would also be limited. The chances were good that if Nicholas was careful, the rogue cop would have to give his position away. But was he still close by?

Nicholas decided to try running to the car to see if he could draw Martin's fire. As he started, two shots sounded and hit the ground close to his feet. As he reached the relative safety of the car, he caught a glimpse of a blue uniform sleeve behind a container two rows behind the car, on the left, back the way they had come. He leaned over the hood and took careful aim.

"Martin!" Nicholas shouted. "Give it up, man, it's all over!"

Martin didn't reply. Nicholas held his aim steady and fired at the sleeve. It quickly moved behind the container.

"Damn!" he said under his breath. Then he said, "Sorry, Madeline." Nicholas figured that he had only grazed Martin's arm, but at least he had let Martin know that he could be killed or wounded just as easily as Martin had shot the other cop. He quickly ran toward the container that Martin was hiding behind and flattened himself against the side.

"Martin! The FBI is on the way right now! If you give yourself up now and speak against Parker, it'll go a lot easier for you!"

Nicholas heard a sound from behind him. Martin had snuck around the container! Nicholas whirled around and fired at the same time that Martin fired. Martin's shot missed Nicholas's head by an inch, and ricocheted off the container with an angry whine. The shot that Nicholas fired hit Martin in the left arm. Martin ran down the length of the container and disappeared around the corner. Nicholas fired again at the man as heran, but he fired too quickly and missed. But his first shot had wounded Martin, and it was bleeding, leaving a trail of blood that Nicholas could follow. The trouble was that Martin would know he was leaving a trail, and he would be watching for Nicholas to come after him.

With no other choice, Nicholas started to follow his prey.

Marcus had called in, letting the Bureau know that shots had been fired, and that there were wounded at the scene. He also told them to be careful coming in because Nicholas was hunting the two remaining rogue cops. The Bureau would be handling the response themselves due to the sensitivity of the involvement of crooked policemen. He hated having to stay in the container to baby-sit the two cops while his friend was facing danger alone. He glanced back at the two. Thankfully, they were fully exercising their right to remain silent. Marcus had a lot to think about.

Nicholas had introduced the little girl as Marcus's goddaughter, and called her Madeline. Her resemblance to Jane was astounding. He could only conclude that she was who Nicky had told him she was. But how could that be? Madeline had died as a fetus. Then, as he watched, she had glowed with a bright light, touched the Richardson girl, glowed again, then both girls faded from sight. The chains holding the Richardson girl had dropped to the floor of the container as if they had passed *through* her.

Marcus had never married, because his job at the Bureau kept him hopping between helping Nicky with his cases, and staying in charge of private security firms that had contracted for jobs with the government, like Joey Justice at Justice Security. His job was his life, and he had hurt a great deal when Jane and the baby had died. He had looked forward to being a godfather.

There was a fountain in one of the city's parks. Marcus privately called it his "wishing well". He had thrown lots of change into the fountain over the last ten years, wishing for peace and happiness for his friend. Had his wishes finally come true?

And, if they had, were they in the form of a ghost?

George Parker was working his way back to the car he had left parked in the rail yard's parking lot. He knew that the place would soon be full of FBI agents, all looking to haul his ass in. He was cursing Nicholas Turner under his breath. How did that son of a bitch know where to find him? Nobody knew that the transfer was today, and nobody knew that he was behind the Richardson kidnapping.

It was the fourth kidnapping he had overseen. When he was contacted to see if he might be interested in providing entertainment for a group of well-off movers and shakers, the money had proven to be outstanding. When added to the money that he had confiscated, collected, and extorted over his years as a cop, a couple of these kidnappings would put him over his personal monetary goal, and he could disappear into South America and live the rest of his life on Easy Street. The Richardson girl was supposed to be his last one.

He didn't care what happened to the ones he kidnapped. As a cop, he had long ago learned to compartmentalize his feelings, and he just didn't think about them after the job was done. Until this job, he had always found some schlepp to do the actual kidnapping, and paid them out of his own pocket. He was going to use that fucking Ricky Logan for this one until he backed out at the last minute. That was all right, though. The contract man he had hired to do Logan and Turner had taken care of Logan. He missed Turner, though...then he died. Too bad for the contract man...but it had saved Parker from taking him out and cleaning up the mess.

Then that damn Martin had shot up the Richardson woman's house, trying to kill her. Instead of taking the fucking heat off, it turned it up...and almost burned his ass! That was okay, though. His cash was offshore and he had a fake passport and ID ready to go. He'd just take off a little sooner than expected. Brazil was calling his name!

He made the final turn and headed for his car. There was a little girl standing there! Was it the Richardson girl? No, this one's hair was brown. She was about the same age, though.

"Hey, kid!" he shouted. "Get away from that car!"

The little girl didn't move. She was staring at him intently, hands at her sides. As he got closer, he saw that she had an angry look on her face. A breeze blew into his face.

"Where's your folks, kid?" No one was in sight. He was within 20 feet of her.

She didn't answer him. Then a thought struck him. The order was for a little girl no more than ten, with blond hair. This one had brown hair, but the age was about the same. Why not snatch this one? He could grab her, throw her into the trunk, make a call, and drop her off himself on his way out of the country, with nobody the wiser. Sure was getting windy!

"Hey, little girl. I'm a policeman, so you're supposed to answer my questions," he said as he closed the distance between them. He looked at her face...if looks could kill! She really had a mad on! Damn this wind!

"Come here, you," he said as he reached for her arm. His hand passed right through her. He looked at his hand as if it was responsible for missing its target, then he looked into the little girl's face. His look of surprise would have been comical had it been anyone else.

The anger in her eyes chilled his spine. "Detective Parker, you're an evil man. You've killed people, you've put people through terrible pain, you kidnapped my stepsister, you tried to kill my stepmother, and you tried to kill my father," she said quietly. "I'm what you might call an angel, Detective Parker. But, *that's my family!*" Her voice became louder. "I AM allowed to have vengeance." Then her voice seemed to come from everywhere at once. "HAVE YOU EVER SEEN AN AVENGING ANGEL?"

Nicholas continued tracking Martin by his blood trail. He had to move slowly in case Martin was waiting to ambush him, and it was getting to him. The path he was following twisted and turned until he felt lost. He was beginning to think that Martin had an endless supply of blood when he began recognizing some of the rows that he was passing through. Martin had circled around and was heading for Marcus and the two cops! Once he realized this, Nicholas began running, still following the trail.

He rounded a row of forty-foot containers and saw Martin standing at the end of the row. Martin was swaying slightly. His left arm was covered with blood. His right hand held his gun, and he didn't seem to know that Nicholas was behind him. Beyond Martin, Nicholas could see Marcus standing just inside the open container. Marcus seemed distracted, and did not see either Nicholas or Martin.

Nicholas crept slowly along the container until he was just a few feet behind Martin. He took careful aim.

"Drop the gun, Martin," he said conversationally. "It's over for you."

Martin seemed not to have heard.

"I don't want to shoot you. Drop the gun."

Martin stopped swaying and began to raise his gun to aim at Marcus.

Nicholas shot Martin in the head.

Marcus whirled toward the sound of the shot, aiming his gun. When he saw Martin fall and Nicholas standing behind him, he pointed his gun upward and ran over to them.

"Looks like you saved my bacon, Nicky."

"Yeah," Nicholas said. "I told him to drop the gun, that I didn't want to shoot him. But he aimed at you anyway. I didn't have a choice."

"Nicky. It's okay, man."

Nicholas nodded. "I know."

The two men heard a thundering voice say, "HAVE YOU EVER SEEN AN AVENGING ANGEL?"

Marcus said, "What the hell was that?"

"My daughter," said Nicholas, as he started running toward the parking lot.

Sparks of pure white energy began springing from Madeline's body as if her body wasn't big enough to hold it. They looked like fireworks as they came out and slowly fell, evaporating before they reached the ground. Her eyes glowed with an intense blue light as her anger grew.

Her voice lowered again, she said to Parker, "The bible says 'Vengeance is mine, saith the Lord', Mr. Parker, but who do you think dispenses vengeance?" She raised her arm, palm pointed at his feet. A white bolt of energy shot from her hand and hit his feet.

The pain was incredible. Parker felt as if his bones were on fire, but there were no visible injuries. He was terrified, and took a step backwards. Madeline followed.

She was talking to him, punctuating each sentence with a white energy bolt. As she walked, more and more of her 'angel' self began to appear. "Sometimes, when it's a really bad person," *FZZT* into his legs. He stepped back again. She followed, and began glowing whitely. "we can take vengeance ourselves." *FZZT* into his stomach. He doubled over and took two steps back. Madeline still followed, and by now her transformation was complete. Her power was cascading into 'wings' again, and her glow was almost blinding. "But, when it comes to my family," *FZZT* into his stomach again. He doubled over again, and noticed a pair of feet standing to his right. He looked up. It was Meredith. "I take vengeance myself!" *FZZZZZZTT !* This shot was all over his body, and the pain was unbearable. The white light from her energy bolt sank into his body with a hiss, searing his soul. He screamed, and reached for Meredith, hoping for some relief.

"NOW, Madeline!" shouted Meredith. Madeline offhandedly threw a white energy bolt at Meredith without taking her eyes off of Parker, bathing Meredith in white light. When the light faded, Meredith was 'real' again.

"Vengeance is mine, saith the Mom," she said, and knocked Parker unconscious with a left hook to the jaw.

Nicholas came into view of the parking lot just as Madeline transformed into her 'angel' self. He barely registered his wonder at her beauty because he was dumbfounded at her display of power. George Parker looked as if needles had been inserted into his body, and, as each bolt of pure white hit him, he flinched as if he had been hit with a baseball bat. Nicholas then noticed Meredith fade in, standing beside Parker. When Madeline used both palms to hit Parker with a huge white bolt, Parker danced as if he had connected with live electricity. Nicholas heard Meredith shout and watched as his daughter threw an energy bolt at Meredith. He watched as Meredith laid Parker out with the most amazing left hook he had ever seen. When Parker hit the ground, Nicholas slowly began walking toward his family, his mouth wide open.

"Close your mouth, Nicholas," said Meredith. "You look like a surprised Howler monkey."

Madeline, who had changed back into her normal self, giggled. "Yeah, Daddy. You look like a surprised Howler monkey...that's trying to use the bathroom!" She giggled again. Meredith laughed, too.

He looked at Meredith and pointed at Parker. "How did you..." he started.

Meredith smiled at him, shaking her left hand. "Madeline softened him up, and I finished him off. Three years of boxing classes at Yale, Nicholas."

Karen faded in on his right side, holding a baseball bat. "Yeah, and I was supposed to be the cleanup hitter," she said seriously, then giggled. "But looks like Parker struck out!"

Nicholas looked at the three women who meant the most to him in his world, and shook his head. "Wow. I hope I never make you three mad."

Sirens sounded in the distance. Nicholas looked back toward the road. "Cavalry's coming. Madeline, change Karen back and *fade*!"

Chapter 9

THE FBI SHUT DOWN THE rail yard and took over the yard office. Everyone told their stories several times, and everyone omitted any reference to Madeline.

With one exception.

Parker sang like a bird to anyone that would listen about the 'angel' that had 'kicked his ass so that the Richardson bitch' could hit him with something big. One of the agents that heard this story pulled Marcus off to the side and said, "It's pretty obvious that he's setting himself up for an insanity defense. I don't see it working."

The one thing Parker wouldn't sing about was the identity of who had hired him. Any time he was asked about it, he would get a frightened look on his face. "My life wouldn't be worth a dime if I tell you that. These people have a long reach and money to burn. I may be a lot of things, but I'm not quite ready to die."

The agents that interviewed Nicholas pressed him hard about where he had gotten his information concerning Karen's whereabouts, but he told them that he had no intention of giving up his informant under any circumstance. Not now and not in court. He told them that the informant had had nothing to do with the kidnapping, and, if pressed, he would say that he deduced it from Logan's information and erratic behavior by Parker, and that there was no informant. One agent that talked to Nicholas threatened to arrest him if he didn't speak. Nicholas lost his temper.

"Arrest ME?" he said. "You want to arrest me after I've solved the kidnapping, caught the kidnappers, and rescued another child? By all means, do it. Right now. And I guarantee that my phone call won't be to a lawyer, it'll be to the media. They'll be all OVER your ass for that one, you pompous asshole! I want to see your supervisor now!"

Nicholas did see the supervising Assistant Director later, and told him what the agent said and what he told the agent. The A. D. apologized to Nicholas, then found the agent that had made the threat. Even though his ass-chewing was behind closed doors, it could be heard all through the yard office.

"Let me tell you something, you sniveling, backstabbing, ladder-climber! If you want a future in this organization, don't you EVER threaten that man again! He's solved more child abductions for this Bureau than my own damned agents! Nicholas Turner, Meredith Richardson, and Marcus Moore should be receiving fucking medals right now! If you'd pull your head out of your ass and work on your cases as well as you threaten civilians, maybe YOU could solve a case or two!"

Several of the people in the rail office were laughing. Nicholas could see Marcus across the room. Marcus's face was beet-red, and he was trying hard to keep himself from bursting with laughter. Nicholas smiled at his friend and gave him a thumbs-up.

Finally, after the interviews were completed, they were all allowed to leave. Someone had retrieved Marcus's car from where it had been parked in the container rows. They all piled into the car, and Marcus started to drive away.

Meredith and Karen were in the back seat, snuggled close to each other. As Marcus drove out of the yard, Madeline faded in beside Karen.

"Hi, kiddo," said Marcus, when he spotted her in the rearview mirror. "I hear you pack a helluva wallop."

"Don't swear, Marcus," said Madeline.

Nicholas burst out laughing at the look on his friend's face. "I've been dealing with that since she showed up, buddy. You might as well give in to it." Nicholas then explained everything about Madeline, from her first appearance, to her appearance in front of McFeely's to get him to save Snickers, to their meeting in his office, the dreams with Jane, and all the way to what happened today. He left nothing out. Nicholas had turned in his seat, so that he could see everyone in the car.

Marcus said, "Wow. So, after ten years, I finally get to be a godfather." He shook his head. "And I can't even tell anybody. That sucks, Nicky. That sucks big donkeys."

Nicholas snickered. "You can tell somebody, Marcus. You can tell my sister about her. Melissa doesn't know yet."

"The hellcat? Not a chance in..." he looked at Madeline in the mirror. "Not happening," he corrected himself. "Nicky, I've got a question, and I'll ask it now, since Meredith has seen what's left afterwards. Are you through with the drinking?"

Nicholas looked at each of the four people in the car with him...or, rather, three people and an angel. Marcus looked concerned, Meredith nodded to him with a slight smile on her face, Karen grinned and winked, and Madeline let her hand glow white as if in a warning. His life had meaning again, and he had no reason to try to forget. He had conquered his personal demons with the help of an angel, and had gained happiness in the conquering.

"Yes, Marcus, I'm done," he said.

They were passing through a block of businesses.

Madeline began grinning.

"Marcus, stop here, would you?" said Nicholas.

Marcus looked at Nicholas, then nodded. "Sure, Nicky." He pulled the car into a slanted parking place. "What's up?"

"I've got to pick up something here," replied Nicholas. "I won't be gone but a minute." He got out of the car and began walking down the street. He turned into a small jewelry store tucked in between a men's clothing store and a furniture store.

"Why's he going in there?" asked Marcus.

Meredith looked at Madeline's grin, then began smiling herself. "I believe he is picking up something for me, Marcus."

Marcus looked at her in the mirror, confused. Then, a knowing look dawned on his face. "Does he know your ring size?"

She nodded, then indicated Madeline as she said, "I think he had a little help from Miss Know-It-All."

Madeline grinned even wider, then Karen started to smile.

"It seems, Marcus, that those two can communicate without saying a word," said Meredith.

"Are you going to say yes?" he asked.

Meredith looked lost in thought. She was quiet for so long that both girls began looking concerned. When Meredith noticed the concerned looks, she smiled.

"Of course I am. I cannot imagine my life without him or Madeline. I love them both, Marcus, and I care a great deal for you, too."

Marcus turned in his seat to look at Meredith.

"I told you he was a keeper, didn't I?"

About The Author: T. M. Bilderback is a former radio announcer with a number of story ideas running around inside his head, most based on, or inspired by, classic songs. The author currently resides in Tennessee, and is writing feverishly in order to banish these stories from his head and into book form, before they drive him screaming into the street.

OTHER WORKS BY T. M. Bilderback

<u>Nicholas Turner</u>
If You Could Read My Mind
<u>Justice Security</u>
Mama Told Me Not To Come
Someone Saved My Life Tonight
Jackie Blue
Wake Me Up Before You Go-Go
Saturday In The Park
MacArthur Park
The Little Drummer Boy
The Night Chicago Died
Jim Dandy
Cow Patty
Hell's Bells
Black Dog
Lido Shuffle
<u>Tales Of Sardis County</u>
Don't Come Around Here No More
Junior's Farm
The Devil's In The Details
I'm Your Boogie Man
<u>Colonel Abernathy's Tales</u>
The Lion Sleeps Tonight
Heart Of Glass
<u>Other Stories</u>
The Wreck Of The Edmund Fitzgerald
Gold
Hot Child In The City
Eli's Coming
<u>Other Novels</u>
Empty Eyes
<u>Story Collections</u>
Greatest Hits